CELTIC
FAIRY TALES
AND LEGENDS

Rosalind Kerven

WARWICK GOB

CELTIC
FAIRY TALES
AND LEGENDS

Rosalind Kerven

First published in the United Kingdom
in 2024 by
Batsford
43 Great Ormond Street
London
WC1N 3HZ

An imprint of B. T. Batsford Holdings Limited

ISBN: 9781849948500

A CIP catalogue record for this book is available from the British Library.

10 9 8 7 6 5 4 3 2 1

Reproduction by Rival Colour Ltd, UK
Printed by Toppan Leefung Ltd, China

This book can be ordered direct from the publisher at
www.batsfordbooks.com, or try your local bookshop.

CONTENTS

Introduction

he stories in this book come from the timeless oral traditions of Ireland, Scotland and Wales.

The oldest and most solemn ones, first written down during the Middle Ages, were once formally recited in the courts of ancient kings by their grandest and most eloquent court poets, as portrayed in a Welsh text of the 14th century:

'My lord,' said Gwydion, 'it is our custom that on the night a visitor arrives at the court of a great man, the chief bard should speak, so I will gladly tell you a tale.' Gwydion was the best storyteller in the world. And that night he entertained the court with pleasant tales and storytelling until he was praised by everyone there.

In contrast, the more light-hearted ones were not recorded in books until the late 19th century or even later. However, they too are very ancient, having been widely shared for countless generations by humble peasants and travelling storytellers around cottage firesides – as described in the western islands of Scotland in 1896:

The arrival of [a storyteller] in a village was an important event. As soon as it became known, there would be a rush to the house where he was lodged, and every available seat

— on bench, table, bed, beam, or the floor — would quickly be appropriated. And then, for hours together ... the storyteller would hold his audience spellbound. During his recitals, the emotions of the reciter were occasionally very strongly excited, as were also those of his listeners, who at one time would be on the verge of tears, at another would give way to loud laughter. There were many of these listeners who believed firmly in all the extravagances narrated.

Despite these very different origins, all the stories retold here have much in common. They are peopled by giants, faeries, dragons, witches, magic animals, bold young women and famous heroes. They tell of astonishing adventures, strange enchantments, impossible ordeals, eerie shapeshifting and visits to supernatural 'otherworlds'. In the words of Irish poet and cultural icon W.B. Yeats, 'Everything exists, everything is true, and the earth is only a little dust under our feet.'

So relax, learn to believe in magic – then read on!

Rest for a while! The night is young,
Time is short and the road is long.
Tell me a story and I'll sing you a song
For tomorrow the road will be calling us on.
– traditional Celtic song

The Sorceress and the Poet

WALES

Where did all the old stories come from? They were gifted to the world long
ago by poets. And who was the greatest poet of ancient times?
To answer that, we must start with a sorceress, the noble lady Caridwen ...

 aridwen was a woman of great power, a renowned mistress of magic.

She was married to a lord and had three children. Her elder son and her only daughter were both as fair as a spring morning. However, it's her youngest child who concerns us. This was a boy called Avagddu, who was born under an ill star.

Caridwen loved Avagddu best of all, but feared he was too feeble to make his way in the world. So she decided to brew a Potion of Inspiration to help him. She hoped this would overcome his disadvantage, enabling him to outshine his rivals and perhaps win a place to serve the king.

She filled a cauldron with rare herbs and water, built a fire in a secret corner of her garden, and set the cauldron on top. Then she commissioned two trusty people to keep it simmering. One was Morda, an elderly serving man who she tasked with feeding the fire with logs. The other was a boy called Gwion Bach. His job was to stir the cauldron with an enormous spoon, every hour, all through each day and night.

'Keep up this work without resting for a whole year,' she ordered them. 'At the end of that time, once the brewing is complete, I shall pay you both generously. But listen: *Do not taste even a single drop of the potion.* If you disobey me, you will die on the spot.'

They diligently obeyed her instructions. For almost twelve months, Morda never let the fire go out and Gwion Bach kept on stirring. Slowly, steadily, the brew became richer and more pungent.

By the last day of the final month, the potion was so thick that Gwion Bach could scarcely move his spoon through it. As he struggled to do so, three drops of the liquid suddenly splashed onto his finger. It was so excruciatingly hot, that he forgot Caridwen's warning and thrust the scalded finger into his mouth to cool. In this way, he accidentally swallowed some of the potion.

Despite her warning, it did not kill him. However, its effect was overwhelming. Almost at once, his head began to explode with a chaos of dazzling images and words. They gushed through him like a river in spate and filled his whole being with desperate longing. He must string them together! He must shape them into prophesies, weave them into stories, shout them out loud as poems and songs! He must work them into spells ...

But old Morda saw what happened and cried, 'You're in mortal trouble now, boy. Quickly, run for your life before Caridwen comes!'

So, his head still ablaze, Gwion Bach fled.

The next moment, the cauldron cracked in two, spilling the remains of the brew into an enormous puddle. But Gwion Bach knew nothing of this as he raced through fields, crawled under hedges and hid in ditches, desperate to escape Caridwen's anger.

She came at dawn the following morning. It should have been the happy day when the potion was finally ready for her son. But instead, she found the cauldron burst, the liquid spilled and the fire reduced to ash. She seized a heavy stake and made to strike the hapless Morda.

However, he stopped her with a roar: 'Don't hit me, foolish woman! It's Gwion Bach who caused this disaster.'

'Then he'll not get away with it!' Caridwen cried.

Power surged through her veins. She sniffed the air, scraped the ground with her naked foot, tested the wind with a raised finger. Thus she quickly divined which way the boy had gone, and started after him.

But thanks to the magic potion, Gwion Bach knew that Caridwen was coming for him. A spell sprang into his mind, he chanted it out loud – and at once transformed into a hare. In this shape he ran on, now three times faster than the wind.

Caridwen saw what he had done. She immediately turned herself into a greyhound, quickly gained on Gwion Bach and drove him to the banks of a rushing river.

Gwion Bach jumped into the water with an eerie cry – and transformed into a fish.

Caridwen turned into an otter, dived in after him and chased him to the surface.

In his fish form, Gwion Bach could not breathe there. So he transformed into a small bird and flew up towards the sky.

Caridwen screeched, turned herself into a peregrine falcon, shot after him like a lightning bolt and harried him hither and thither.

Gwion Bach flew through the open door of a barn, transformed into a grain of wheat and hid amongst thousands of identical grains scattered across the floor.

Caridwen cackled, knowing she had him cornered now. She turned herself into a hen and scratched around the floor. It did not take her long to find the grain that was really Gwion Bach, peck him up and swallow him.

*****

Nine months passed. The lady Caridwen gave birth to her fourth child. It was another boy, conceived from the grain of wheat she had eaten – her enemy Gwion Bach himself, come back to life!

She could not bring herself to harm him. So she gave him a new name, Taliesin. Then she wrapped him in a leather bag and entrusted him to God's care by casting him out to sea.

What became of Caridwen and her other children after that is not recorded. But of Gwion Bach, now reborn as Taliesin and set adrift, there is much more to tell.

*****

Further up the coast, there lived a young lord called Elffin.

One evening, he went out riding along the river to the estuary, where a weir had been set up to trap fish. A leather bag was snarled up in one of the poles. Elffin thought it might contain something valuable, so he untangled and then opened it. To his astonishment, he found nothing inside but a tiny boy. It was the strangest child he had ever seen: the size of a newborn baby, but with the physique of a youth.

When Elffin had recovered from the shock, he carefully placed the boy on the ground. There, like yeast dough left in a warm place, he rapidly began to grow.

'Who are you?' Elffin cried in astonishment. 'Where have you come from?'

The boy, now as high as Elffin's waist, only grinned at him, pointing silently at the horse.

'Do you wish to come home with me?' asked Elffin.

The boy had now grown to reach Elffin's shoulder. A nod was his reply.

Elffin lifted him onto the saddle behind him and they started off at a trot. As they went, the boy suddenly broke his silence and began to chant in a curious, mesmerizing voice:

> *Greetings, friend! Taliesin's my name*
> *I drank the potion, fled in shame*
> *From the sorceress Caridwen*
> *Devoured by her then born again.*
> *Generous man who set me free —*
> *I thank you for my liberty!*

Elffin had no idea what he was talking about; yet there was something appealing about the fey boy. When they reached the family home, Elffin's parents too were charmed and offered to foster the boy. Under their care, he flourished, while a canon of enigmatic poems grew inside his head.

*****

Time went by, as it does, and Taliesin matured into a man. One day, Elffin invited Taliesin to join him at a feast thrown by their ruler, King Maelgwn of Gwynedd.

Halfway through the feast, Maelgwn summoned his bards to step forward and perform. They recited an endless series of praise poems to their king, followed by a tedious history starting with his most distant ancestors, rumbling on and on. All the guests sat there politely, desperately trying to hide their boredom and impatience.

Suddenly, Elffin rose from his seat, pointed at Taliesin and shouted: 'Enough of these humdrum verses! Your majesty, I have a bard of my own who is far more skilful than yours. His poems will fill you with wonder. You should hear him!'

King Maelgwn was outraged at this audacity. He ordered Elffin to be seized, thrown into the dungeon and confined there in chains. In the commotion, Taliesin tried to dart away and conceal himself; but he was quickly spotted in the shadows, dragged out and forced to stand before the king.

'So,' Maelgwn growled. 'You must be the wretched rhymester who my prisoner dared to claim is superior to my own world-famous bards, eh?'

Taliesin stood glaring at Maelgwn brazenly for a long moment. Then he cleared his throat and made his answer in verse:

> *Indeed, sir! Taliesin's my name.*
> *The whole world soon will know my fame.*
> *Lord king, I stand here not for sport.*
> *I'd like to entertain your court,*

But first it falls to prove to you
What Elffin claimed is really true.
Throughout the world, outside or in,
The greatest bard is Taliesin.
No peace will come till you agree.
Restore my brother's liberty!

'How dare you tell me what to do!' cried Maelgwn. Taliesin's reply was a grim warning:

Lord king, don't argue but beware!
For danger's coming from out there:
A monster's rising from the mud,
No flesh, no soul, no bones, no blood.
Brings teeming rain and glowering skies
The sea will churn, the wind shall rise.
Merciless, it's sure to bring
Dark vengeance on you, foolish king!

The next moment, there was a deafening clap of thunder outside, followed by gusts of wind so strong that they rattled the heavy doors and windows in their frames, enveloping the entire hall in an icy chill. Rain and hailstones drummed against the walls and roof slates as if they would batter the whole castle right down.

Above this clamour rose the king's distraught voice, pleading: 'Taliesin, call off this spell at once! I submit to you! I agree to free Elffin and will declare you to be the greatest poet in the land. I offer humble apologies for doubting your skills. I beg you to join my court as chief bard. Will you accept?'

'Certainly!' Taliesin called back.

'Then subdue this tempest, I implore you! Save my castle from destruction!'

Taliesin snapped his fingers, muttering a stream of words under his breath in a language that no one recognized. Gradually, the noise outside quietened, the rain ceased and the wind faded away.

'It is done,' said Taliesin. 'Now take me to Elffin, my foster-brother, and let me oversee his release.'

The king himself led the way down steep, dank steps to the dungeon. Behind them came workmen with saws to break the chains binding the captive's wrists and ankles. But before they could start work, Taliesin spread out his hands to stop them, stepped forward and cried at the top of his voice:

> *Let me speak my magic art:*
> *Chains of bondage — break apart!*

At once the chains melted clean away, and Elffin stepped out of them.

The king shook his head in astonishment, then led the way back up the steps, with Taliesin and Elffin walking directly behind him. At the top, they found the royal bards waiting in line to pay homage to their new chief. Taliesin stood quietly to receive their acclaim.

After this, the feast was concluded, heralding the king's customary time to enjoy some bardic poetry. This time, none dared to speak except for Taliesin himself.

Standing on the dais before the assembled guests, he no longer looked like a reckless youth. Instead, he now had the bearing of a sagacious dignitary; and the words he spoke were profound, complexly crafted in open verse:

> *Friends: I bring you mysteries to ponder.*
> *Why is a stone hard and a thorn sharp?*
> *Who is all at once hard as flint, salty like brine and sweet as honey?*
> *Whose steed is a gale?*
> *Why is a wheel round?*

Which is whiter, salt or snow?
Why is a tongue gifted with speech?
What is lovelier than the sun's smile?

No one could offer answers to these mysterious questions, and Taliesin did not enlighten them.

In this way, the evening drew to a tranquil end. Then the entire court and the king's guests all bedded down in the great hall around the fire.

They awoke the next morning to a new era, in which the art of poetry and the stories it shapes had gained equal status to the art of war. So it has been in the Celtic lands ever since; and the name of Taliesin the bard has never been forgotten.

The Swan Woman

IRELAND

nder the white mist lie the green hills. Within the green hills stand the stone doors. Behind the stone doors lie the *sídh*, castles of the Otherworld. They illuminate the underground realms just as the full moon brightens the night; for within them stand the dazzling courts of the Tuatha Dé Danaan, the gods of ancient Ireland.

*****

In a chamber within one of these *sídh*, the god Aonghus lay fast asleep.

Music broke into his dreams. He opened his eyes with jolt, and saw to his amazement that a young woman was standing by his bed. How had she come there? Who was she? Her long pale fingers were stroking the strings of a timpán, making a tune so agonizingly sweet that it almost tore his heart in two. Never before had he seen or heard such beauty.

He stretched out a hand to touch her; but she shook her head with a smile and shifted beyond his reach.

On and on her tune rippled, pouring over him like a brimming mountain stream. He was too overcome to reach out to her again, or to utter a single word. Finally, intoxicated by both her face and the music, his eyes flickered shut and he succumbed again to sleep.

They say there is no disease or even pain in the Otherworld. Yet the next morning, Aonghus woke up paralyzed with yearning, too ill to rise from his bed.

He could not tell anyone the cause of it, fearing he would be mocked. For Aonghus was the god of love, charged with helping and supporting both gods and mortals who find themselves hopelessly smitten; he should not succumb to such weak feelings himself. Yet here he now was, laid helpless by a woman whose name he did not know, whose very existence seemed like a dream.

He withdrew from everything. He ceased his habitual travelling through the two worlds, he abandoned hunting and feasting, he no longer gave anyone romantic assistance. Instead, he wasted away in his bed all day, not eating and scarcely drinking. Now he lived only for the nightly blessing of sleep, which always brought back the unknown woman and her exquisite timpán music to delight him.

*****

Aonghus' father was The Dagdae, a powerful Otherworld king. After his son had idled away a whole year in this way, he summoned doctors to examine him. Eventually, they correctly diagnosed the cause of his affliction. Aonghus was compelled to confess to his father about the young woman who haunted his waking dreams.

The Dagdae said, 'My son, I well understand your desperation, for I myself once coveted an unobtainable woman in a similar way. She was none other than your own mother! But it only took some simple enchantment to persuade her to love me.'

'Perhaps the young woman you love acts so clandestinely because she is similarly prohibited from becoming your wife. In that case, I advise you to use the same method which once worked so well for me.'

Aonghus answered, 'You make it sound like a simple matter, Father; but your advice only increases my wretchedness. For even the strongest spells are bound to fail against a woman whose name, father and dwelling place are all a mystery.'

'That is no reason for despair, my son,' said The Dagdae. 'I shall send messengers to seek her out and discover everything you need to know about her. I promise not to rest until this is achieved. Then you can easily go to her and reward her surreptitious advances by offering your own affection.'

And so it was done.

After many months had passed, a neighbouring king of the *sídh* called Bodb came to Aonghus' bedchamber, saying, 'Rise up, my friend! I have found the woman you love. She is called Cáer Ibormeith, daughter of Ethan Anbúail, and they live in the province of Connachter.'

'Then they are mortals?' Aonghus asked.

'They are indeed,' said Bodb. 'Even so, it won't be easy to overcome the father's selfish hold on her.'

'Is he a mighty king?'

'Not a king,' said Bodb, 'but a powerful enchanter.'

'Is it through her father's spells that she comes to haunt my dreams?' asked Aonghus.

Bodb's answer was ambiguous. 'It seems she does this in secret opposition to her father's will. Yet he holds far more sway over her than you can imagine, Aonghus. To overcome his spells, you must first understand them. And to do this, you must come to their realm and see the situation for yourself.'

*****

It was already late in the year. Summer had long ago faded, the leaves had dropped and the nights were drawing in when Aonghus rose from his bed. He joined King Bodb in his chariot and drove with him beyond the boundaries of the Otherworld, all the way to Ethan Anbúail's kingdom. However, instead of approaching the palace there, they continued their journey through pasture and forest to the shores of a tranquil lake.

There they saw an extraordinary sight. Thrice-fifty young women in pure white dresses were standing knee-deep in the clear water; and each was joined to the one beside her by a gleaming silver chain.

Aonghus gazed at them. He examined the chained women carefully, one by one ... and suddenly blenched. When he managed to speak, his voice was barely a groan: 'There: I see her!'

He pointed to the woman in the very centre of the lake. She was a full head taller than her companions; and the heavy chains that weighed down her shoulders and circled her neck were not silver, but crafted from burnished gold.

Bodb said, 'Now you can clearly see why it will not be so easy to win her. Besides, come midnight, you may not even want her.'

'Midnight?' said Aonghus; and there was fear in his voice.

'You have slept too long,' Bodb said sharply. 'Do you not realize? Tonight is Samhain – the first day of winter, the turn of the year, the time of changes. So tonight the door between this frail human world and our sacred Otherworld will swing wide open. And for a brief time even mortals will have power to spin spells so strong that we gods are helpless before them. Wait here and watch: you will see what her father is capable of.'

Without another word, he returned to his chariot and drove off, leaving Aonghus alone at the water's edge.

Slowly the sun dipped behind the forest in a blaze of blood-red light. The air grew cold. Stars shone in the dark sky like fragments of silver, lighting the thrice-fifty young women swaying and murmuring in the water. Aonghus watched them, transfixed by the tall one in her chains of gold. As the darkness thickened, her father's evil magic took hold and she began to change ...

... Curved breast to coiled neck. Draped robe to white feathers. Alluring mouth to proud beak. Fingers that once danced across the timpán lost in the fold of wings ...

Cáer had become a swan.

The links of her golden chains were broken. She rose into the air surrounded by her flock, thrice-fifty ladies who were now, like her, transformed to the great white birds of air and water. Long necks extended, together they soared and circled above him, then turned to fly away.

'Cáer!' he shouted. 'Wait!'

From high above, her sweet voice tumbled back to him: 'Who calls me? Who is there?'

'I am Aonghus of the Tuatha Dé Danaan,' he answered.

He heard a flutter of wings, saw her turn back from her companions to hover high above him.

'Aonghus. I thought you did not really care for me. But you found your way here at last.'

'Every night for a year you haunted my dreams, Cáer,' he called back to her. 'Every day for a year after that, people on my behalf have scoured the two worlds in search of you.'

She gave a bitter laugh. 'And now you see that the search was pointless, Aonghus. It is impossible for you to win me from my father. Indeed, you cannot even want me now, unless you wish to marry a bird. My father has vowed never to let me go, and has thus bewitched me to take this swan shape on alternate years, right to the end of my life.'

'That is no impediment to my love for you, Cáer! Come to me and I will show you.'

'If I come, you must understand that until next Samhain my nature is not of a woman, but a swan. I will need neither a soft bed nor treasure, but only sky and water.'

'I understand, Cáer!' he cried, 'and I promise to respect you.'

She descended to the starlit lake and glided towards him. He stood very still, waiting. When she reached the bank, he waded out and put his arms about her.

And as they embraced, he too began to change, just as she had done only moments before, shimmering and dissolving into a storm of snow-white feathers, until he became a swan.

The thrice-fifty swan-maidens once set to guard Cáer had already vanished.

Aonghus spread his new-fledged wings and rose into the sky. Soon he was soaring beside Cáer, high above the darkness and the Samhain fires. Then Cáer and Aonghus together began to sing. Their voices carried right across the world so that all who heard them were lulled into an enchanted sleep for three long days and nights.

Thus unseen, Aonghus in his swan shape flew home to the green hills with Cáer beside him. He led her through a great stone door, beyond the darkness, into the splendour of his *sídh*. There, safe inside the Otherworld, her father's enchantment lost all its power, and Cáer returned to her true shape. Aonghus too transformed, back to a lusty god. In this way, the pair were now free to love each other for ever.

Mally Whuppy and the Giant

SCOTLAND

here was once a poor woman and her husband who had far more children than they could possibly feed. So, in desperation, they took three of their daughters deep into the forest and used trickery and deceit to leave them there.

By the time the girls realized they were abandoned, night was falling. There were no other people around, the owls were screeching, the wolves were howling and they had no idea where they were. The two elder girls sank to the spot and started to weep bitterly.

But the youngest one – Mally Whuppy they called her – was a shrewd and plucky lass. 'What's the point in mewling?' she said. 'Look, the moon's shining and there's a path through the trees. It must lead somewhere, so let's follow it until we reach a house. We can ask there for help.'

So hand in hand, they started along the path. Before they had gone very far, they saw lamplight ahead and soon reached a high-walled cottage. Mally Whuppy knocked hard on the door, which was opened at once by a timid-looking woman.

'What do you want?' said she.

'Please, ma'am, we're lost,' said Mally Whuppy. 'May we come in to sleep by your fire tonight?'

'Och, you poor bairns,' said the woman. 'I've got three daughters of my own and I'd help you if I could – but I was forced to marry a wicked giant – and he'll kill you when he comes home!'

Mally Whuppy peered past her and saw a table set with huge loaves of bread and jugs of milk. Her empty stomach rumbled. 'We're starving,' she said. 'Could you at least spare us something to eat?'

'I'll have to be quick,' said the woman nervously. 'I suppose you can come in and get warm for a few moments while I fetch something.'

She beckoned them in to kneel by the fire. The woman's own sullen-looking daughters – who looked as big and brutish as their father sounded – sat on stools opposite them, scowling. The woman bustled off and quickly returned with a bundle of food wrapped in a cloth.

But before she could hand it to Mally Whuppy, they heard heavy footsteps outside. Then the door burst wide open – and the giant himself came stooping through it. Huge as a bear, he was, wearing a thick leather belt studded with metal spurs; and his breath stank of sour beer and blood.

At once, he spotted Mally Whuppy and her sisters. 'Why are these mortals soiling my home?' he roared at his wife.

'Och, they're just three poor cold and hungry lassies who stopped by,' she said soothingly. 'Don't worry, they're going now.'

The giant bent down to peer at them closely. A dangerous gleam came into his eye. 'Going? Hmm, there's no need for that. It will do us good to have company, heh, heh, heh! You're welcome – *very* welcome! – to sup with us, dear girls, and fatten yourselves up. Then I'll be glad – *very* glad, heh, heh, heh! – to have you stay the night. You can sleep in the same bed as my own three, there's plenty of room.'

So Mally Whuppy and her sisters joined the giant and his family around the table, and they had never eaten so well in all their short lives. Once they had finished, it was bedtime. The giant's daughters climbed a ladder up to the loft and got into one side of a large bed covered in crisp white linen. Then, with sly grins, they invited Mally Whuppy and her sisters to lie on the other side. Soon after that, the giant came up to bid them 'good night' and placed a chain of gold around each of his daughters' necks. Then, chuckling under his breath, he adorned Mally Whuppy and her sisters with necklaces of straw.

Soon the two elder sisters were lost in slumber, as were the giant's smug daughters. But Mally Whuppy had the sense to keep pinching herself to ensure she stayed awake. She thus heard the giant descending the ladder, his bed creaking when he got into it, and the deafening sound of his snores. She got up and surreptitiously swapped things around, taking the gold chains for her sisters and herself, and putting the straw necklaces around the giant's daughters. With that done, she got back under the covers and lay very still, wide awake and waiting.

In the middle of the night – *stomp, stomp, stomp* – the giant came up to the loft again and made for the bed. His huge hands groped their way across the six girls. When he felt the straw necklaces now worn by his three daughters, he dragged them out, hurled them to the floor and beat them until they lay dead. Then he hurried back down the ladder, muttering to himself: 'Fresh human girl steaks for breakfast in the morning, heh, heh, heh!'

The clamour woke Mally Whuppy's sisters, who lay frozen and mute with fear. Mally Whuppy told them in hasty whispers what had happened and how she had saved them.

'Quickly,' she urged, 'we must escape while the giant's sleeping off his frenzy!'

So the three crept down the ladder, out of the door, into the forest, and along the path again, running as fast as they could. On and on they hastened, so that by the time the sun was rising on a bright new morning, they were standing in front of the king's palace.

The guards were outraged to see three scrawny, ragged girls loitering by the gates and tried to shoo them away. But bold Mally Whuppy stood with arms akimbo, looked them in the eye and said, 'Take us to the king! We've got something important to tell him.'

She was so persuasive that the guards ushered them straight into the royal hall. There the two elder sisters stood back while Mally Whuppy curtsied before the king, saying, 'Your majesty, we've just escaped the evil giant of the forest!'

'Really?' said the king. 'That's extraordinary. I've never heard of anyone escaping him before. Tell me exactly what happened.'

So Mally Whuppy did.

When she had finished, the king said, 'Mally Whuppy, you sound like the very person I've been looking for. Would you be willing to do me a favour?'

Mally Whuppy winked at her sisters and said, 'It depends on what kind of reward you're offering.'

'If you do what I ask,' said the king, 'you can have my eldest son to marry your eldest sister. Then you and your middle sister can live with them in comfort and luxury for the rest of your lives.'

'Hmm,' said Mally Whuppy. 'That sounds a fair bargain. What do you want me to do?'

'Go back alone to the giant's house,' said the king, 'and steal the sword that he hangs at night above his bed. If you're not too afraid, that is.'

'Of course I'm not afraid!' said Mally Whuppy. And she set out to do the daring deed at once.

She ran down the path all the way back to the giant's house, cautiously opened the door and peeped in. No one was there. So she crept inside and hid under the giant's own bed.

Shortly afterwards, the giant's wife came home; and shortly after *that*, in stomped the giant himself, whistling cheerfully. He hung up his sword and joined his wife at the table to eat a hearty supper. Mally Whuppy tried not to think what kind of meat was in their stewpot. Then they went to bed.

As soon as both were snoring, Mally Whuppy emerged from her hiding place, surreptitiously stretched her arm above the bed, and removed the sword from its hook. However, as she pulled it towards her, it knocked against the bedhead with a loud *CLANG*! – which immediately wakened the giant.

He sat up with a start to see her scuttling out of the door, dragging his huge sword behind her. Out of bed he jumped and started after her. Mally Whuppy ran for her life. Closer and closer came the giant …

And that would have been the end of her, had not the path suddenly led to a wide, bottomless chasm. The only way over it was a bridge as narrow as a single hair. Mally Whuppy was so skinny from hunger that she easily managed to squeeze along it. The giant, however, was far too big and heavy to follow.

'Don't you dare come back!' he roared after her, 'or I'll pulp you to mincemeat on the spot!'

Mally Whuppy didn't stop to answer, but hastened back to the palace. There she presented the sword to the king; and very pleased he was to get his hands on it.

'Well done, Mally Whuppy,' he said. 'I'll start preparing the wedding between my eldest son and your eldest sister straightaway. Meanwhile, would you do another job for me? If you do, your middle sister can marry my middle son.'

'Of course,' said Mally Whuppy. 'Tell me what you want and I'll do it at once.'

'I'd like you to bring me the giant's purse,' said the king.

'And where will I find that?' said Mally Whuppy.

'It's out of reach during the day,' said the king, 'because he wears it between the sharp metal spurs on his belt. But at night he keeps it under his pillow.'

'Right,' said Mally Whuppy, 'I'll see you tomorrow then.' And she ran back to the giant's house, sneaked in and hid under the bed again. There she waited until the giant and his wife had finished another abominable meal and gone to sleep. Then she crept from her hiding place, silently reached under the giant's pillow and pulled out his purse. However, as she carried it away, she couldn't help knocking it against the doorframe, making the coins inside it jingle loudly – which again awakened the giant.

Out of bed he jumped and chased after her, with Mally Whuppy running for her life until she reached the bridge as narrow as a single hair.

Again she went nimbly across it, leaving the giant unable to follow, and beside himself with rage.

'If you dare come back a third time,' he roared after her, 'I'll thread you on a skewer and toss you to roast on the fire!'

Mally Whuppy ignored him and raced back to the palace, where she handed the purse to the king; and very pleased he was with it.

'Well done, Mally Whuppy,' he said. 'That's two weddings to prepare now. Would you run one final errand for me? If so, you shall have the greatest prize of all for yourself: my youngest and most handsome son.'

'What must I do to win him?' said Mally Whuppy.

'Pull the ring off the giant's finger,' said the king.

So Mally Whuppy ran back to the giant's house, where she hid under the bed yet again. As soon as the giant and his wife had settled down to sleep, she emerged from her hiding place, crawled lightly across the covers, took hold of the giant's enormous, hairy hand and gently tugged the ring off his finger.

But this time it was not so easy to get a head start on the giant. Because as soon as the ring came free, he jerked awake and grabbed her!

'Caught you at last, Mally Whuppy!' he roared. He held her up close to his face so that her legs were dangling and her arms flailing in the foul stink of his breath. 'I'm going to fetch my thickest, sharpest cudgel to beat you to a pulp, then skewer your remains for roasting.'

He shoved her inside a sack, tied up the top, hammered a strong nail into the wall, hung the sack from it, then went outside for his cudgel.

Mally Whuppy peeped through the sackcloth. She saw the giant's wife getting out of bed and immediately had an idea. 'Whooh, whooh, whooh!' she shouted at the top of her voice. 'You should see the wonderful things inside this sack!'

'What things are those, Mally Whuppy?' asked the giant's wife.

Mally Whuppy didn't answer but kept shouting: 'How beautiful they are! Such treasures!'

This turned the giant's wife wild with curiosity. 'Show me them before my husband comes back,' she called, 'I beg you!'

'They're certainly well worth seeing,' said Mally Whuppy. 'But are you sure you want to risk it? You'll have to climb inside here, which will put you in terrible danger.'

'I don't care! I've got to see them and I'm sure I've got time,' the giant's wife insisted.

'All right,' said Mally Whuppy. 'Let's swap places.'

So the giant's wife helped Mally Whuppy out of the sack and climbed into it herself.

'I can't see anything,' the giant's wife complained.

Mally Whuppy ignored her, for she was busy hiding behind the door – only just in time, as the giant came stomping back, brandishing a huge cudgel covered in sharp thorns.

'Right, Mally Whuppy,' he roared, 'you'll get it now!'

His terrified wife tried screaming and yelling that it was now *her* in the sack, instead of Mally Whuppy. However, the dogs in the kennel outside were all barking so loudly that the giant could not hear.

Then Mally Whuppy felt guilty, because she remembered how the giant's wife had tried to be kind when she and her sisters first arrived at the house. So before the giant could start beating the sack, she sprang from her hiding place, made sure he saw her, then dashed out of the door.

In a fury, the giant made to go after her. However, at that moment his wife's struggles loosened the sack from its hook, sending her tumbling to the floor inside it – and he tripped over her. By the time he was back on his feet, Mally Whuppy had already crossed the bridge as narrow as a single hair.

Looking behind her, how she laughed at the sight of the giant raging impotently on the opposite side! Then she scampered back to the palace, where she presented the giant's ring to the king.

'Well, Mally Whuppy,' said the king, 'that's three impossible tasks you've completed. You certainly deserve your reward.'

He now introduced her to his youngest son, who turned out to be not just handsome, but also as warm-hearted as Mally Whuppy herself was brave. They fell in love instantly. So the wedding preparations were now expanded yet again, enabling the three humble sisters all to get married at the same time to the three royal princes, followed by a magnificent feast and dancing right through the night.

Afterwards, Mally Whuppy and her sisters quickly adapted to royal life in all its bounty. They lived in great comfort and joy for the rest of their lives.

The Devil, the Witch and the Faeries

WALES

n a pleasant green valley, there once lived a young woman who was courted by a man claiming to be a gentleman farmer. Her parents did not approve, for they felt there was something both unsavoury and uncanny about him. However, the young woman ignored their advice and, despite their efforts to stop her, continued to meet him in secret. Well, that suited the gentleman farmer perfectly, because it enabled him to present her with a gift that he knew her parents would burn at once if they saw it. This gift was a book called *The Dark Arts*, and its subject was witchcraft.

The young woman was fascinated by it. She kept it hidden under her bed and read it by candlelight in the small hours of each night while her parents were fast asleep, making steady progress with her studies. This pleased her suitor so much that eventually he decided to trust her with his great secret: He was not really a farmer, but none other than the Devil himself in disguise!

'Oh, that's fine by me,' said the young woman nonchalantly. 'In fact, I had my suspicions that was who you really are, though I didn't like to ask.

So what happens next?'

'Now you've learned the arts of witchcraft, we can make a deal,' said the Devil.

'What kind of a deal?' she asked.

'I'm a generous fellow,' he said, 'so I'll offer you a choice. You can have either seven years of unlimited money; or seven years of unlimited magic power over other people.'

The young woman considered this carefully. 'I'll take the magic power over others, if that's all right by you,' said she. 'There's a number of people in this village who really annoy me, so it would be fun to put some painful spells on them. What happens after the seven years?'

'You will become my property,' said the Devil smoothly. 'Which means I can torture you at my pleasure until the end of time.'

Of course, the young woman should have guessed as much, but hearing it stated so plainly brought her up with a start. Stammering, she told the Devil she had changed her mind and no longer wanted to strike a bargain with him. But he insisted the deal was already sealed, and it was too late to cancel it.

To silence her complaints, he built her a house – or rather, it built itself by his magic – and set her up in it. He also gave her two smaller but more specific gifts. One was a crooked magic staff to draw her enemies into her power. The other was a magic witching ring in the grass in front of the house, which he paced out with his cloven hooves. Once the staff had brought her enemies there, they would be forced to stand helplessly inside this ring while she bewitched them.

Naturally, the young woman's parents tried their best to stop her from leaving home, but once again she ignored them. She soon got going in her new role, put aside her last reservations and for a while greatly enjoyed herself. She started with some village girls who she'd always envied because their clothes were more fashionable than hers. Once her staff had drawn them into her magic ring, she caused their ankles to twist, their knee joints to tear and their toes to break so they could scarcely walk. Next came a youth who had once rejected her flirtatious advances: she charmed an ugly, twisting horn to grow on his forehead, making him look like a monster. Then there was an old lady who got her back up by mocking the young woman's weed-infested yard. She found herself forced to stand in the witching ring until misty films had grown over her eyes, sending her almost blind.

When the victims managed to limp home, they all blamed the young woman for their afflictions, and everyone believed them. However, no one could do anything about it, because she was rarely seen outside, and the house the Devil had built for her was impenetrable.

*****

After this had gone on for a long time and countless people had been plagued by her spells, a great change came to the valley. A troop of faeries suddenly arrived, sixty of them or more, led by one they called the Queen of the Dell. They settled next to a clear spring that bubbled out of the hillside, building a palace for the queen on the upper slopes, and a big house which the rest of them shared below. When they were finished, the queen went to a nearby patch of grass and used her wand to draw three magic rings of her own on it – *faery* rings – one inside another.

By this time, the villagers were heartily sick of magic and they waited nervously to see what the faeries would do. But they had no need to worry, for the next day the faeries paid friendly calls on their new neighbours. 'We heard you've been having problems with witchcraft round here,' they said. 'So we've come to help you by rooting out the evil one and destroying their power.'

'Oh, we all know who's behind our problems,' they said; and they told the faeries about the tragic case of the young woman who had sold her soul to the Devil in return for the gift of evil magic.

The next day, the Queen of the Dell invited the witchcraft victims to visit her at the spring. When they arrived, she asked them to stand together inside the central faery ring. All the faeries then lined up within the middle ring, and marched in pairs around the victims, chanting in a strange tongue that none of the villagers understood. Then the queen went into her palace, leaving the doors wide open, sat on her throne and asked the victims to form a queue. One by one, she called them up, touched them lightly on the head with her wand, then sent them to bathe in the spring three times. When they emerged, dripping with sparkling water, they were all completely cured of their afflictions.

They went to kneel before the Queen of the Dell, exclaiming loudly in gratitude.

'I'm glad my remedy was successful,' she said gently. 'Now go home, put on dry clothes and get on with enjoying life, while I deal with the witch.'

*****

By then, the seven years that the Devil had granted the young woman for mischief had almost passed. Continual malice had ruined the young woman's appearance; whereas before she had been quite attractive, now she had the sour face and menacing posture of witches you might have seen depicted in old books. To tell the truth, she was no longer enjoying herself at all; and she lived in dread of what the Devil would do once he claimed her for his own.

Then she heard how the Queen of the Dell had broken her spells and restored her victims to good health. Was it possible, she wondered, that this good faery might be persuaded to help her too, despite her wickedness? She summoned up her last dregs of courage and paid the queen a visit.

To her surprise, the queen received her warmly and invited her into the palace. She was so easy to talk to that the young woman found herself confessing everything: how she had defied her parents to consort with the Devil; how she had diligently studied his book of dark arts; and of the cruel bargain they had struck, enabling her to harm innocent people simply because she disliked them.

'I can see you're ashamed of yourself,' said the Queen of the Dell. 'So let's find a way to change things. Come back here tomorrow morning with the book and the crooked staff he gave you, and we'll see what we can do.'

The young witch woman arrived as soon as dawn broke. She found everything already prepared for her, with a merry fire blazing away right in the centre of the inner ring. A pair of faeries took her hand and led her to stand by the flames, telling her to wait there. Shortly after that, the Queen of the Dell emerged from her palace, brimming with power drawn from sitting on her throne all night. She walked into the outer ring and began to step slowly around it, following the direction of the sun, and muttering inaudibly under her breath. Suddenly, she stopped, raised her arms high and beckoned to the other faeries.

They formed a long line and began to march around the middle ring circling the young woman, who was now quaking from head to toe. As they moved, they repeated the queen's mystical words over and over.

The words faded away. The Queen of the Dell walked round the outer ring until she was directly facing the young woman. 'Cast your book and staff of evil into the fire,' she said.

At first, it was as if the young woman's fingers were glued to these two tools of witchcraft, for she could not let go of them. But at last, with great effort, she managed to hurl them both into the flames.

At once, they flared up: yellow, red and white-hot, with a clap of thunder that shuddered through the surrounding hills and mountains. The next moment, the fire was overwhelmed by a mass of dancing, screeching shapes: demons!

'Sing, my faeries!' the Queen of the Dell cried. 'Together we can overcome them!'

The faeries continued to move around their ring, their voices now raised in melodious chanting. The demons surged around them. The queen strode past the demons right up to the fire, which was now dying down into a column of thick grey smoke, and reached out with her wand. The smoke subsided to reveal a heap of smouldering embers and ashes. The young woman was crouching beside it, holding her head in her hands.

The queen stepped past her and raked the ashes with her wand, carefully searching through them. At last, she said softly to the young woman, 'The Devil's book and the crooked staff he gave you are all completely burned. Nothing remains of them. Wait here while I finish my work.'

The demons were still darting around the outer ring above the faeries, close enough to see their fiery breath streaming out, yet always just beyond reach.

'Go!' the queen commanded them, brandishing her wand. 'Leave the Earth! Return to your own infernal abode! And I command your master to release this young woman who he tricked into his power.'

The sky darkened. There was an ominous stillness, like the calm before a storm.

'I cast you all away from here!' cried the queen. 'Go, I say again, go!'

The demons suddenly rose into the air like a flock of crows. There came another thunderclap. The ground shifted beneath their feet. The demons merged together into a single dense, colourless ball of evil … burst into a blinding shower of dust … drifted to the ground … then melted away like snow on a warm day.

Slowly, slowly, the air cleared again.

As the demonic dust vanished, so did the young woman's witchery. She stumbled to her feet, blinking and swaying, gazing humbly at the Queen of the Dell, who now walked across the rings to meet her.

'Oh, my lady, thank you!' the young woman exclaimed. She dropped to one knee and held out her hands like one who is praying. 'You've saved me! I wish for nothing now except for you to let me serve you in return.'

'Nothing would please me more,' the queen replied with a smile.

She beckoned the young woman to follow her out of the rings and into her palace. There she reached under her throne and pulled out a purse and a glass bottle.

'Take these,' she said. 'The purse is filled with gold. Use it to buy enough simple food to keep yourself fit and well, then donate the rest to people who are too frail to work. The bottle contains a secret mixture of faery herbs mixed with water from the sacred well here. It will heal people and also help mothers endure the pains of childbirth. I wish you

to serve me by using it on anyone who asks for it; rich people should pay, but treat poor people for free. So long as you use both purse and bottle as instructed, each morning when you wake up, you will always find them completely full again.'

'I promise to do exactly as you say,' the young woman replied meekly. 'Also, I promise never to hurt anyone ever again. Today, I must start by healing the ones that I ...' she looked down in shame '... that I harmed with the Devil's witchcraft.'

'That wicked time is over now for good,' said the Queen of the Dell. 'For your life is reborn, and you must take a new name. From now on, everyone will know you as Madam Dorothy and sing your praises as a great healer.'

'Are you going to stay here to watch over me?' asked the young woman.

'No, we faeries have finished our work here,' said the queen. 'So let us say goodbye, for it's time for us to move to another place where we are needed.'

She shook the young woman's hand and led her outside. There the other faeries ran up, formed a circle of linked hands and moved solemnly around her, performing another song of enchantment. Then they rose into the air. As her eyes followed them, they gradually shrank until they were no bigger than thistledown. A sudden gust of wind blew them all away.

*****

That was the end of both the Devil and the faeries. But it was just the beginning for Madam Dorothy, whose astonishing generosity and medicinal skills soon made her famous throughout the land.

Fionn mac Cumhaill and the Magic Drinking Horn

IRELAND

f ever there was a warrior whose aim was so true that just the sight of his spear sent enemies bolting in terror, it was Fionn mac Cumhaill, leader of the High King's men, the Fianna. And if ever there was a leader whose wisdom and generosity equalled that of a thousand sages, that was Fionn mac Cumhaill too. So you'll not be surprised to learn that whenever Fionn led his men out hunting, exceptional sport was guaranteed.

However, there had never been a hunt like this one before. For the stag that leaped from a thicket into the sunshine had no less than twenty-four sharp points on its antlers, towering over them like some creature from the Otherworld. At a yell from Fionn, the hounds began to chase it, with all his men galloping after. Across bogs, over rocks, up hills and through deep-cut glens they went, scarcely pausing for breath; yet still the stag raced on, with such speed and grace it seemed almost to be flying. As the sun sank behind the mountains, one by one the Fianna abandoned the chase, until only two were left. One was Dara the musician. The other, of course, was Fionn himself.

As for the stag: on a high hilltop it suddenly vanished into a wood.

Fionn and Dara dismounted and began beating about the tangled undergrowth, trying to flush out their prey. But they had no success. It was now not only getting dark, but also a mist was rapidly descending. Within moments, they could no longer see their horses or, indeed, each other.

'Dara!' Fionn called. 'There's something uncanny about this mist. And that stag we've been chasing: I'm sure it's no natural creature. Some enemy must be trying to confuse us. We'd best stay where we are and sit this out. Sing out the war-cry, so the others know where we are.'

Dara put his hands to his mouth and bellowed out a sonorous, warbling sound, carrying far across the valley. Several answering cries came back, but they sounded very far off and quickly faded away.

'Listen!' said Fionn suddenly. 'Can you hear a woman's voice, wailing?'

'Another trick?' said Dara.

'Possibly,' said Fionn. 'But whoever it is sounds in deep distress. It would be shameful to ignore it.'

They walked towards the sound, shoulder to shoulder through the swirling vapour, until they made out a shadowy figure, which spun round in alarm at their approach. They saw she was a young noblewoman, her rich clothes badly torn and covered in mud.

They stopped a few paces away and Fionn introduced themselves.

'So it's Fionn mac Cumhaill yourself, is it?' she cried, sounding annoyed rather than impressed to meet the great hero. 'Well, Fionn, it's all because of your men that I'm lost in this dreadful faery mist. My husband heard your hunting horns while we were crossing the mountains here – such a distinctive sound they make – and he got so excited that he ran off to try and find your band. "I can't miss an opportunity to meet the famous Fianna!" he told me. "Don't worry, I'll be back in no time." "Huh!" I shouted after him, "Knowing you, I'll be lucky to see you before next week." So I tried to follow the path on my own. But this weird mist suddenly came down, and now I can't even tell which way I'm facing.'

'Good lady,' said Fionn, 'I humbly apologize that we led your husband astray, and I'm afraid we haven't seen him. Will you allow us to escort you to safety?'

'Of course,' she said. 'That's one of your jobs, isn't it? – to help women in trouble. My name's Glanlua, by the way. Please, let's be on our way.'

The three set off together. The path had vanished, so they walked carefully, side by side, down a slope of grass and loose scree. However, they seemed to make no progress, with the slope stretching on and on like a bad dream.

Eventually, Glanlua said, 'I'm sorry, I'm exhausted, I can't go any further.' With these words, her knees gave way and she swooned.

The next moment, Dara too sank to the ground, and closed his eyes; then even Fionn could not help but lie down beside him ...

*****

They all awoke at the same time. The mist had entirely lifted, the sky was blue and the weather had turned pleasantly warm. They were no longer on the hill, but sitting by a large lake. On the bank immediately opposite them was a splendid stone castle.

As they stared at it, a man and a woman came out of the castle door, plunged into the lake fully dressed and swam rapidly towards them. They hauled themselves out onto the bank – and revealed themselves as giants!

Fionn staggered to his feet and went to meet them.

'So you got here at last, Fionn mac Cumhaill!' the giant man roared. 'Fionn "the *mighty*", I've heard them call you. In that case, why do you look as pale as a pot of sour whey?'

'Your magic is certainly effective,' said Fionn, 'but I'll soon get over it. Who are you?'

The giant man laughed. 'Dryantore's my name.' He pointed at the woman beside him, who was almost as tall and stout as he was. 'This is my sister Ailna. Now, I suppose you want to know why we've taken such extreme measures to capture you, eh? It's because of the Battle of

Knokanare, when you killed Ailna's husband, and my two sons. This is our revenge.'

'Ah ... Yes, I remember that battle,' said Fionn. 'Naturally, you're grieving for your dead kin, but I was forced to kill them in order to defend my own people.'

'That's neither here nor there,' said Dryantore. 'Vengeance is our due and we're going to take it.'

He clapped his hands. A troop of gigantic guards came running up, so brawny that even Fionn could not resist them. In no time, the three were tied up in ropes, and dragged through the icy water to the far shore. Here their feet and hands were bound with iron fetters. Then they were pushed down a steep stone stairway into a dungeon.

*****

They spent the night incarcerated there, with neither food nor drink. Naturally, Fionn and Dara treated Glanlua with utmost decorum.

In the morning, the door atop the dungeon steps opened, and the giantess Ailna made her way down to them.

'I trust you all slept well,' she said sarcastically.

'Perfectly,' was Fionn's reply.

'I wish you hadn't,' said Ailna. 'And I heartily wish the rest of the Fianna were locked up here too. As for you, Lady Glanlua, aren't you mortified to be with the despicable Fianna?'

'I only met up with them completely by chance,' said Glanlua coolly, 'because I was lost in the magic mist that you and your brother sent, up on the hills.'

'Is that so?' said Ailna. 'Well then, I suppose I shouldn't punish you for *their* wicked deeds. And I could do with some female company. I tell you what: wait here a little longer, while I consult with my brother.'

She went back up the steps, locking the door behind her. Shortly afterwards, Dryantore himself came down, freed Glanlua from her shackles with his bare hands and carried her from the dungeon.

'May we meet again in happier circumstances!' she called behind her.

'The best of luck to you!' Fionn and Dara shouted back.

In the main hall of his castle, Dryantore sat her at a grand table, laid with the finest spread of food you could imagine. But the enchanted mist, combined with incarceration, had left Glanlua too weak to eat. She closed her eyes, leaned back and again fell into a swoon.

When she came round, Ailna was leaning over her, holding out a golden object. 'This is my special magic drinking horn,' she said. 'A single sip from it will make you feel better at once.'

Glanlua accepted the horn, tipped it into her mouth and swallowed the sweet liquid it contained. Almost instantly, her strength returned. She now tucked into the meal with relish; but as soon as she had finished, she remembered her erstwhile companions, still shut up underground, with neither food nor drink.

She spoke of this to Ailna and Dryantore, who were both seated at the table watching her.

'They're staying in the dungeon until I'm ready to kill them,' snarled Dryantore.

'But you won't enjoy the fun of killing them if they die beforehand of thirst and starvation,' Glanlua pointed out.

The giants admitted the sense of this. So Ailna took Glanlua back to the dungeon, and allowed her to deliver bowls of stale bread and water to Fionn and Dara – just enough to keep them alive. Glanlua wept to see these great men fallen so low; but giantess Ailna guffawed at them.

Back in the hall, Dryantore told Glanlua to sit down, then started firing questions at her:

'Who's the little fellow with that wretch Fionn?' he asked her.

'I think they call him Dara,' said Glanlua. 'I don't know anything about him; as I said, we only just met.'

'You must know something,' Dryantore growled. 'Or do you want to go back to the dungeon?'

'Well ...' said Glanlua, thinking quickly. 'Er ... I've heard talk that he's supposed to be the Fianna's best musician, if that's of any help.'

'Hmm,' said Dryantore. 'My sister and I could both do with some music to lift our spirits.'

He stomped down to the cellar and thrust open the iron door. 'You, Dara!' he roared. 'Sing for me.'

Dara exchanged glances with Fionn, then answered in a barely audible croak, 'I'm afraid I can't, Dryantore. Your barbarous treatment has taken away my voice.'

'Then I might as well slaughter you now,' growled Dryantore.

'If you lend me a timpán, I could probably manage to play a tune for you,' croaked Dara. 'But you'd have to give me proper sustenance first, because at the moment I don't even have strength to move my fingers.'

So Dryantore had Dara dragged up to the hall and fed more bread and water. Then a timpán was brought to him. With considerable effort he managed to play a very fine tune on it; then stopped abruptly.

'Keep playing,' Dryantore growled, tossing him another hunk of bread. 'Or I'll throw you back in the dungeon.'

So Dara's tune went on and on, getting louder and louder ... In fact, it grew so loud that it was heard by the other Fianna, who were still searching for Fionn and Dara on the mountain. They instantly recognized Dara's style of playing, and followed the sound until they reached the far shore of the lake from the castle. Suspecting Fionn and Dara had been taken captive there, they swam across the water, hunting spears at the ready to attack any enemies who came to meet them.

But as soon as they reached the far shore, the giant enveloped them in his magic mist. They too became disorientated, lost all strength, collapsed and were dragged into the dungeon. Thus, in great wretchedness, they were reunited with Fionn.

A short time later, Dara was hurled back down the steps to join them. And here they all remained, totally helpless, with barely enough bread and water to stay alive.

The next morning, Dryantore came crashing down the dungeon steps, waving his outsized sword, swaggering amongst the stupefied men, who were all unable to lift even a single finger in self-defence. He attacked them randomly, until the dark hole was awash with their blood and echoing with their groans.

Finally, he grew tired of tormenting them and went away.

Once the door had slammed behind him, Dara spoke up: 'Fionn and the rest of you, listen. When I was upstairs in the castle playing the timpán, I saw Glanlua. She was in good health, with all her beauty restored. She managed to sneak over to me and revealed the secret of her recovery. It's a magic drinking horn containing an antidote to Dryantore's spells. If we could get hold of it and all drink from it, we'd be able to destroy the brutes and escape.'

Fionn said, 'But how can we obtain this horn?'

One of the men, Conan, groaned, 'I'm half-dead here, Fionn, but I reckon I could turn that to our advantage. When the brute comes back, leave it to me.'

Soon they heard Dryantore's boots on the way down to the dungeon.

Before the giant could say anything, Conan called to him falteringly. 'Lord Dryantore! Look at my back: the skin's hanging off in shreds and I'm slowly bleeding to death. But if you'd heal these wounds, I'll volunteer to be your slave! I'm not afraid of hard work, and Fionn mac Cumhaill here will vouch for my honesty and strength. I'll labour all day and all night for you for nothing – for ever! – if you'll spare me.'

Dryantore sniffed. 'A slave, eh? Unlimited work and nothing in return for it? Let me see what my sister thinks.'

He went back upstairs then soon returned, bringing a large, shaggy sheepskin. 'Ailna says, if I put this over your injuries, they'll heal,' he said.

He draped the sheepskin over the wounded man's back. Sure enough, at once, Conan's wounds all vanished, and he was no longer in pain. However, the sheepskin seemed to be permanently stuck to his skin and impossible to throw off.

'You'll have to work for me like that, shaggy-shanks,' Dryantore guffawed at him. 'And if you don't like it, or can't carry out all the tasks I set you, I'll slaughter you as previously planned.'

Conan winked surreptitiously to the others. To Dryantore he said, 'Thank you, sir. Right, take me upstairs and I'll do everything you tell me.'

The pair went up the steps together.

A short while later, Dryantore came back. 'You: Dara,' he roared. 'That Conan fellow's been telling me more about what a good musician you are. He reminded me I won't get the chance to hear you playing after I've killed you. So I've brought the timpán, to make the most of you while I can.' He thrust it at Dara. 'Play me some tunes on it – now!'

Despite his rapidly diminishing strength, somehow Dara managed to pluck the strings. Gradually, the music took him over with its own subtle magic, until he was managing to perform as splendidly as he had ever done when fit and well. The magic infected Dryantore too; he began tapping his foot in time to it, nodding and swaying. Dara played on …

… Until the dungeon door suddenly opened again. They saw Conan, still wrapped in the sheepskin, and heard him call down, 'Dryantore, sir!

Your sister, Lady Ailna, has sent me to you. She can't find your magic drinking horn anywhere, and wants you to find it.'

'It's where I always keep it,' Dryantore snarled.

'She says it's not, sir. She needs you to come up at once.'

'Ach! Very well. You, Dara! You're to play more as soon as I come back. As for you, shaggy-shanks, get out of my way!' He strode upstairs, pushing Conan aside – and leaving the door at the top swinging open.

Conan waited for the giant's footsteps to fade away and then, grinning broadly, flung back the sheepskin. From its folds, he pulled out the magic drinking horn.

'Here it is!' he cried. 'When I was upstairs, Glanlua managed to point out where Ailna hides it. As you heard, I managed to convince Dryantore to get a last taste of Dara's music. As soon as he was out of the way, Glanlua distracted Ailna, giving me the chance to grab the horn. Dryantore will spend ages hunting all over his hall for it and arguing with his sister. So let's all drink from it at once – then make our escape.'

He passed the horn into Fionn's hands for the first taste of the enchanted liquor. Fionn took no more than he should, then quickly passed it around his men. As each one recovered, he drew the sword from his belt, ready to fight.

Scarcely had the last one finished than Dryantore appeared at the top of the steps. He stood there for a long moment, amazed, then yelled, 'Ailna, bring reinforcements!'

They heard the giantess running along the passage to the door above … saw her stop beside her brother, turn pale with alarm…then come tumbling down the steps, hitting her head hard against the dungeon wall and the stone floor… And at last, she moved no more.

Dryantore gave a long bellow of rage. Then he drew his sword and flew down the steps. But the Fianna were ready for him. They attacked him from every side, until the giant was on his knees, begging for mercy. Fionn mac Cumhaill stepped forward and struck the final blow.

As Dryantore keeled over, the Fianna gave three great whoops of joy. Then Fionn led them up the steps and into the castle. There they found

Glanlua waiting for them. With a smile, she led them to a long table, already set for a feast with golden dishes, piled high with meat and all manner of other good foods.

'Sit down,' she said. 'The giants had prepared this to celebrate Dryantore's final victory of killing you all, one by one. Well, now it's right that you should celebrate *your* victory over *him* instead. Eat! Drink! Let us all be merry!'

So they did, and it's no lie to say that never had any warriors been in such need of feasting, or enjoyed their food so much. Afterwards, they went to sleep stretched out on soft couches, too satiated to consider how to find their way home.

And as it turned out, they had no need to worry. For when they woke the next morning, they were not in the giants' castle – but lying on the mountainside, next to the very spot where the deer they'd been chasing had vanished; and the morning sun was shining on them brightly.

Kate Crackernuts

SCOTLAND

here was once a king's daughter – Katherine by name – whose mother died too young, leaving her to live alone with her father. He was an indifferent, busy man and she longed for a proper companion.

Eventually, the king took a second wife, a widowed noblewoman. She too had a daughter who was slightly younger than Katherine, and went by the name of Kate. As soon as they met, the two stepsisters became soulmates and were almost inseparable.

The new queen, however, was a jealous, scheming woman. She greatly resented Katherine, fearing that her superior beauty and royal birth meant her own daughter would always be treated as second best.

The more the queen thought about this, the angrier she became. So one night when the king was away, she went out covertly to visit an old hen-wife reputed to be skilled in working evil enchantments.

The hen-wife immediately realized the identity of her clandestine visitor and was greatly honoured. 'Of course I can help you, ma'am,' she cackled. 'Send your hated stepdaughter to me at first light tomorrow, and

I'll deal with her to your satisfaction.'

The queen thanked her, promised excellent payment and rose to leave. But the hen-wife stayed her, saying, 'Wait, madam, and listen carefully. In order for the charm I have planned to work, your stepdaughter must arrive here very hungry. Forbid her to have even a taste of food before she comes.'

The queen assured her she would do this, and hurried back to the castle. The next morning, she woke the two girls at dawn and, while they were dressing, called Katherine to her side. 'My dear,' she said with a false smile, 'I need you to carry out an errand. Cook tells me we have no eggs left for breakfast. The kitchen maid has been taken ill, so *you* must run to the old hen-wife up the road and fetch some.' She gave Katherine a basket, ushered her to the castle door and sent her on her way.

However, Katherine felt too light-headed from lack of food to walk. So she sneaked round to the castle pantry and helped herself to a large slice of cake. Thus fortified, she hurried to the hen-wife's cottage and innocently asked for the eggs.

The hen-wife perceived at once that she had eaten – which meant the evil spell she had planned would not work. So she directed Katherine to the pot where she kept her eggs, saying, 'Help yourself. And when you take them to your stepmother, hinny, tell her from me to close the door more tightly behind you next time.'

Katherine did exactly as told. When she got home and repeated the mysterious message, the queen realized that the girl had managed to get hold of some food. So the next day, on exactly the same errand, she walked her all the way out of the castle gates, ordering the guards not to let Katherine back in until she had brought the eggs.

Poor Katherine's stomach rumbled and she felt weaker than ever. Fortunately, as she staggered along, she saw some peasants picking peas in a field beside the road and persuaded them to give her a large handful. Eating these again protected her from the hen-wife's spell, enabling her to return home with both the eggs and the same message for the queen.

So on the third day, the queen accompanied Katherine all the way to the hen-wife's cottage, leaving the poor girl no chance at all to satisfy her appetite. The hen-wife greeted them both warmly, saying to Katherine, 'Go to the egg-pot, my dear, and help yourself as usual.'

But as soon as Katherine lifted the lid off the pot, something dreadful happened. Her head fell off her neck and rolled away across the floor! And a sheep's head grew in its place!

Katherine had been such a bonny girl before. But now she had a mottled grey snout, yellow eyes and a pair of twisting, crinkled horns! The queen laughed heartily at her, thanked the hen-wife for her excellent service, paid her generously and strode home. Katherine, meanwhile, could not even weep, since her eyes were now those of a sheep instead of a human. She crawled across the floor, picked up her own head, and sorrowfully crammed it into the egg basket. Then, feeling hungrier and more wretched than ever, she slowly made her way back to the castle, constantly dodging behind trees and hedges whenever she saw someone approaching, for fear of being mocked.

Luckily, she could still speak, though in a grotesque, bleating voice, so once she got home, she was able to tell Kate exactly what had happened.

Kate, of course, was horrified. 'Don't worry, sister!' she cried. 'I promise that whatever happens, I'll always look after you. Oh, how I hate my wicked mother for doing this! I refuse to ever see her again. Here, let me wrap your new head in this big silken scarf so no one can see it. Then we'll leave the castle together and make new lives for ourselves.'

So hand in hand, the two girls went out into the world.

*****

They walked further than is possible to imagine. At last, they reached the gates of a palace that was twice as big and twice as grand as their father's castle.

'I'll ask for a job here,' said Kate. 'Hopefully, if I work really hard, they'll pay me enough to keep both of us in comfort.'

'But when they see your sister has a sheep's head,' said Katherine, 'they'll want nothing to do with you and send you away.'

'No, they won't,' said Kate, 'because they'll never find out so long as you keep the scarf on and stay silent.'

The two girls went round to knock on the servants' door, which was opened by the housekeeper.

'Good morning, ma'am,' said Kate. 'I'm a hard worker and I've come to offer you my services. As payment, all I ask for is simple lodgings and a little food for both myself and my poor sister here. As you can see, she has to keep her face covered, because she suffers terrible headaches, which leave her unable to speak.'

The housekeeper clucked with sympathy when she heard of Katherine's condition and looked Kate carefully up and down. 'It sounds as if you're well-used to dealing with illness, eh?' said she. 'So yes, I can indeed offer you a job. That's if you're not put off by it and can manage to stay up all night. You see, the king's eldest son is also ill. He's been in bed for weeks with a mysterious disease that puts him in a terrible, filthy sweat every morning, too exhausted to get up, and then he spends all day dozing. The king's consulted the best doctors in the land, but they all say it's impossible to cure him until he's been watched carefully right through the night to discover the cause of his symptoms. Every servant here – including me – has tried to do this, but we all end up quickly falling asleep in his bedchamber. If you could stay awake beside him all night and find out what's making him so ill, his father the king would reward you well. Meanwhile, I can find a quiet corner for your sister to rest in while you do this.'

Thus it was agreed. Early in the evening, while Katherine rested in a box room, the housekeeper took Kate upstairs to meet the prince in his bedchamber. Despite his pale face and dark-ringed eyes, Kate saw at once that he was an impressive young man. He nodded indifferently at her then sank back on his pillows with a groan and went back to sleep.

The housekeeper lit a single candle then left them alone. To ensure she herself did not succumb to slumber, Kate kept rising from her chair and pacing around the room. In this way, the evening progressed calmly, until a distant clock struck midnight.

At once, everything changed!

The prince suddenly pushed off the covers and stood up, fully alert, eyes shining. He pulled on his clothes and boots, opened the door and hastened downstairs. Walking on tiptoe, Kate followed. Out through the main door they went, across the courtyard to the stable. There he saddled his horse, led it out and mounted it.

Unnoticed, Kate jumped lightly up onto the saddle behind him; and they galloped away into the woods. As they pushed their way through the overgrown trees, Kate's shoulder brushed against a large bunch of dangling hazelnuts. She reached up, pulled them off and slipped them into the pouch on her belt, thinking they would be good to eat if she was out for a long time.

They emerged from the wood onto the open moor, hastening towards a large hillock. Here the prince drew to a halt, dismounted and hissed: 'Open, green hill! Allow this prince to enter!'

Thinking fast, Kate added her own whispered command: 'And let this lady enter too!'

With a soft creak, a large, upright slab of stone slid to one side, revealing darkness. Beyond it was a dazzle of lights. The prince tethered his horse, then stepped into the opening. Kate followed. The next moment, the stone door closed behind them.

One behind the other, they emerged into a magnificent, rose-scented hall, lit by hundreds of lamps in iron sconces. A crowd of ethereal youths and girls were dancing there to the music of pipes and fiddles, singing in

eerie voices.

Kate drew in her breath. This was surely the realm of faeries!

Two of them spotted the prince and drew him into the dance. At once, he was transformed, capering around wildly with them, and laughing at the top of his voice as if he had never been ill.

Kate withdrew into the shadows and perched on a low rock to watch the dancers. As she watched the dancing, a small faery boy appeared out of nowhere and started skipping tantalizingly to and fro before her, brandishing a wand. At that moment, she heard a passing dancer remark languidly to his partner, 'Why ever doesn't that king's daughter snatch the wand? Is she too stupid to realize that a single stroke of it would free her sister from bewitchment?'

As soon as she heard this, Kate drew out two of the hazelnuts she had gathered on her journey and rolled them ostentatiously along the floor towards the faery boy. With a squeal of delight, he chased after them, dropping the wand in his eagerness. Kate snatched it up and concealed it under her cloak ...

She was not a moment too soon. For, at the same time, a cock crowed outside – and at once all the faery dancers melted away like mist. The prince, left alone, spun round in a circle, then rushed down the dark tunnel, back to the stone door. Kate slipped along after him. When the slab opened at his command, she followed him out and again got surreptitiously onto the horse behind him. They galloped all the way back to the palace, where he tumbled into bed and at once fell asleep, dirty and dishevelled, dripping with sweat.

Kate found her way to the little room where Katherine too was asleep, in her horrible sheep's head. Kate gently stroked the wand across her. At once, Katherine awoke and, to both girls' joy, her normal head was restored in all its glory.

They now went together to the prince's fireside, where they sat cracking the remaining hazelnuts, eating them for a simple breakfast. A little later, the housekeeper came in to ask how Kate had got on.

'I've discovered the cause of the prince's illness,' she replied. 'It's possible I could even find out how to cure him if you'll allow me another night or two.'

Naturally, the housekeeper readily agreed to let Kate stay on. Meanwhile, she was charmed to meet Katherine, who said she felt much better after her rest, and offered to do any kind of work needed in the palace.

The next night passed in exactly the same way, except that this time there was no sign of the faery boy in the mound.

On the third night, while Kate watched the prince in his frenzy amongst the dancers, the faery boy ambled by with a bird perched on his hand.

This time, a passing dancer remarked, 'Let's hope that king's daughter doesn't steal the bird and feed it to the prince!'

'Indeed,' said her companion. 'Because then we'd lose our power over him and he'd escape.'

As soon as they had moved on, Kate jumped up and repeated her trick of rolling hazelnuts conspicuously in front of the faery boy. He was so excited as he ran after them, that he dashed the bird carelessly to the floor. There it fluttered briefly then lay still. Kate snatched it up and carried it under her cloak back to the palace at cockcrow, behind the prince.

Katherine was waiting for them in his room. As the prince collapsed into bed, Kate showed her sister the dead bird and repeated what the dancers had said. Together the two girls plucked it, stoked up the fire and set it to cook over the flames.

The scent of cooking caused the prince to stir. He called out weakly, 'I'm so hungry! If only I could taste whatever is making those delicious smells.'

'So you shall,' Kate called back.

She removed the roasted bird from the flames onto the hearth, broke off a morsel of flesh, took it to the prince and placed it delicately into his mouth. Slowly, still in a trance, he managed to chew it. A little colour flowed into his drawn face. He sat up and asked for more.

By the time he had finished the last morsel, all his vigour had returned. He leaped from his bed and seized Kate's hand, thanking her with all his heart for saving him.

'But tell me who you are, he cried. 'Who is the other girl with you, and what brought you both here?'

So now all three of them sat by the fire. Kate shared out the remaining hazelnuts while the two girls told him their extraordinary story. Then it was the prince's turn to reveal how he had been bewitched by the faeries. But at that moment, the door flew open to admit the housekeeper, followed by the king himself and another equally impressive-looking prince.

The king took in the scene before him: Kate cracking nuts around the fire, with his eldest son now looking the picture of good health and talking animatedly with the girls. 'Good gracious, Kate Crackernuts,' he cried, 'you have done what everyone else found impossible: you have cured my eldest son! You must have a huge bag of gold at once. And – if you both

wish – you may marry him.'

'Thank you, sir,' said Kate. 'I'd like that very much.'

'And so would I,' exclaimed the prince.

Meanwhile, as soon as Katherine and the younger prince set eyes on each other, they too fell in love. So a double wedding was held, though neither Katherine's indifferent father nor Kate's cruel mother were invited.

And so, as the old storytellers say, unless they have died since then, both couples are still living happily ever after.

The Red Dragon

WALES

ong ago, in the days when history was preserved only in poems, and magic was a respectable profession, there lived a British king called Vortigen. His reign was a terribly troubled one, for he was constantly harassed by brutal invaders, who eventually forced him to retreat to the peaks of Mount Eryri in Wales.

There, he commissioned stonemasons to build him a fortified tower strong enough to withstand even his fiercest enemies. They began work at once. By sunset on the first day, the foundations were already dug and the first stones of the outer walls laid in place.

However, Vortigen's bad luck was far from over. For when the builders returned at dawn the next day, they found the stones had crumbled to dust, the foundations had collapsed, and all their tools had vanished. Exactly the same thing happened on the following day, and on the third day too.

In desperation, King Vortigen sought advice from every quarter, and thus discovered that amongst his new Welsh neighbours were a number of

highly respected wizards. He summoned them all to come urgently to his camp.

The wizards carefully examined the blighted site, then consulted together in private. At length, their leader went to Vortigen, bowed deeply before him and said, 'My lord the king, together we have gazed into the past, the future and even further into the Otherworld. In this way, we have discovered how to stop the constant destruction of your tower. You must send messengers throughout the land, to seek out a young boy who has no mortal father. Bring him here; then kill him with your own sword. After that, your builders must dig the foundations yet again, then sprinkle the dead boy's blood over their work. That will appease the evil forces which are causing this trouble. Then your proposed stronghold will stand firm and quickly be completed.'

Vortigen was greatly puzzled. For though scoundrels often disown children they have fathered out of wedlock, no child can possibly grow in his mother's womb unless a mortal man sows the seed. Nevertheless, he sent messengers to hunt through all the cottages, farms, villages and towns of Wales, just in case they could find such an unlikely boy.

At first, none had any success. But towards the end of the third day, one of the messengers came to the city of Carmarthen and sat down wearily outside the gates to rest. It so happened that a gang of lads were playing ball nearby, and a quarrel suddenly broke out between two of them.

'Everyone knows you're a despicable bastard!' one of them cried. 'That's why you're so useless!'

'I'm far superior to an ignoramus like you!' the other retorted.

'You can't possibly be,' said the first lad. 'You don't have a father of any kind!'

At these words, the messenger leaped to his feet. But the boys had already scampered away through the city gates. He went after them, stopping to ask the gatekeeper: 'Do you know the boy without a father who just passed through?'

The gatekeeper laughed. 'Everyone knows that loudmouth; he can't keep his crazy thoughts to himself.'

'Does his mother live here?'

'Yes, she does, poor woman. She's the unmarried youngest daughter of the King of Dyfed, but he cast her out for bringing double shame on the family.'

'For having an illegitimate child?'

'Exactly. But even worse than that, she refused to name the man who seduced her, instead claiming she was impregnated by what she calls "supernatural means".'

'My friend,' said the messenger in great excitement, 'if you tell me where this boy and his mother can be found, I will pay you well.' He unhooked the purse from his belt and held it open, revealing the clutch of gold coins that Vortigen had given him for that purpose.

The gatekeeper held out his hand greedily, saying, 'They both live in the city nunnery.'

The messenger gave him generous payment. The gatekeeper not only admitted him into the city, but also directed him to the office of the chief magistrate. There the messenger told of King Vortigen's search for a fatherless boy, saying that he understood such a boy could be found in the local nunnery. He discreetly made no mention of what that boy's fate was to be. The magistrate knew the townspeople would be glad to see the back of the disgraced lady and her arrogant young son. So he arranged for the pair to be taken by wagon to Vortigen's camp on Mount Eryri without delay.

*****

When they arrived, Vortigen welcomed them with a grand feast befitting the lady's status as a king's daughter. As they sat back afterwards to the strains of harp music, he asked the lady about her son's origins.

Her eyes glazed over; then she spoke frankly, in a soft and pensive voice. 'It was all very strange. One day, while I was seated in my private chamber at my father's castle, a great drowsiness came over me. So I sent away my damsels in order to get some rest. As I lay back on my couch, I suddenly saw a young nobleman – a complete stranger – standing beside me. I had no idea how he could have entered, for my father always insisted that my door was kept locked and guarded by two strong men; and suitors were forbidden to visit without a chaperone. I found it a welcome treat to be alone with such a handsome and courteous man. We talked for some time, finding we had much to say to each other; and when he took me in his arms and kissed me, I confess I did not resist. However, to my great alarm, while we were embracing, he seemed to melt away like snow under the sun, until he had completely vanished. I never saw him again, though the memory of him filled both my dreams and my waking solitude for many months. Then one day I realized I had conceived a child. So my father banished me, for shame, to the nunnery in Carmarthen where yesterday your messenger found me.'

Vortigen narrowed his eyes at her. 'So you cannot name an actual man, either living or dead, who could have fathered your son?'

'I cannot, sir,' she answered with a wistful smile. 'His father is definitely the handsome ghost who continues to haunt me – not just in my dreams, but also in my son's own face.'

Vortigen, in a turmoil of excitement, summoned back the wizards and repeated what he had heard.

'Can this really be true?' he demanded.

'My lord the king, it can indeed,' their chief replied. 'For it is recorded in the ancient books that, on rare occasions, children may indeed be conceived in the curious way this lady described to you. There are spirits that exist in the hazy realms between the moon and the earth, with the nature of both angels and men. They are called *incubus dæmons*. When the whim takes them, they are known to assume human shape and beguile naive young women. From what she told you, it was surely one of these who put this lady with child. You have fulfilled your difficult quest to find a boy who truly has no mortal father!'

All this time, the boy himself had been left alone, dumped in a corner like a bag of turnips and excluded from the conversation. Nevertheless, he heard everything said about him, by both his mother and the wizard chief.

Now he came forward and, without even bothering to bow, said brazenly to the king, 'Sir, what do you want of me?'

Vortigen was too discomfited to answer.

The boy said, 'I don't need you to tell me, for I have worked it out already. You intend to kill me, then sprinkle my blood on the foundations of your constantly broken fortress. You hope this will make it stand firm. Is that not so?'

Vortigen could not deny it.

The boy went on, 'The wizards who instructed you to do this have given bad advice. It will not work.'

'Who are you to criticize the greatest minds in Wales?' Vortigen exclaimed. 'Guards, seize this urchin and bind him in ropes!'

However, before they could move, the boy cried, 'Wait! Listen! You ask who I am. My name is Merlin. You claim that I understand nothing. Yet only *I* can reveal the true cause of the nightly destruction of your unfinished fortress.'

Vortigen was so taken aback that he allowed young Merlin to accompany him and his counsellors to the ruined foundations.

When everyone was assembled there, Merlin did not wait for permission, but began to issue further audacious instructions. 'My lord the king, order your labourers to dig up all the soil in the centre of this spot. When they strike water, tell them to keep digging until they have completely uncovered a deep pool.'

This was done. At length a pool of water, dark and still, was exposed below the intended centre of the tower.

Merlin now said, 'Tell your workmen to dig conduits all around the pool and let the water completely drain away.'

Again this was done. At the bottom, balanced on top of the quagmire, two huge earthenware pots could be seen.

'Remove the pots,' said Merlin. 'Under the spot where they are standing, you will find a tent. You must unfold this, but very carefully, for two dragons are sleeping inside it. Stand well back, let them awaken naturally, then watch what they do.'

The workmen heaved the pots away and gingerly unfolded the tent, revealing two sleeping dragons, as Merlin had predicted. They darted out of the way to join King Vortigen and his wizards, who were all watching from a safe distance.

One of the dragons was white, the other red.

At first, both were motionless. But as the fresh air washed over them, their eyes opened, they stretched and rose to their feet. Sturdy as boulders they were, with wings twice the size of an eagle's, forked tongues, and talons like curved knives. Even Merlin flinched from them. However, the dragons had no interest in anything but each other. Within moments, in a haze of billowing smoke and blinding flames, they had begun to fight.

Never had such a contest been seen before within the shores of Britain; and never will its like ever take place again. At first, the white dragon had the ascendancy. It seized its opponent in its claws and hurled it around the drained pool, trying to drive it over the rim to be smashed against the craggy cliffs below. But at the last moment, the red dragon managed to force the white one back towards the opposite edge. Then the white one gave a snort of fire and pounced on the red one again. Three times this happened, while the spectators all cried out in awe and terror, wondering how it would end.

The red dragon was surely growing weaker, for it sat huddled in a corner, cowering and trembling. At any moment the white one was bound to fully destroy it ...

But this turned out to be a pretence – for suddenly the red dragon reared up with a screech that almost split the mountains asunder. It spread its wings, soared into the air ... then plunged down on top of the white dragon. It forced it through the cracked earth below the drained pool – and thence to the depths of Hell.

Thunder rumbled amidst a dazzle of lightning. The victorious red dragon soared up to the highest peak. There it seemed to double in size, again blinding the spectators with its smoke and flames; and by the time the air cleared, it too had vanished.

'What does this mean?' King Vortigen demanded of his wizards. But even their eminent chief shook his head, mystified.

'Allow my son to tell you,' said the lady softly.

Merlin stepped directly in front of the king. 'Sir,' he said. 'The red dragon is a symbol of your oppressed people. You saw how it overcame the white one, which represents the evil invaders who expelled you from your previous strongholds. The red dragon's victory shows that all is not lost. For have you not come to the most splendid realm in Britain? Are not its green valleys overflowing with meat, milk and honey? Just as the red dragon finally drove out the white one and destroyed it, one day you too will destroy your enemies.'

When he heard this, King Vortigen exclaimed loudly in praise of Merlin.

*****

Allowing Merlin to guide him, Vortigen led his followers away from the blighted mountain peaks and successfully built a new fortress in a fertile valley. He engaged artists to paint a prominent red dragon onto all his banners, to inspire his warriors to victory. After that, he carried out many great deeds and was victorious in a long series of battles.

In the end, he was killed by poison.

As for Merlin, Vortigen offered him a large plot of land, telling him to build his own city there. However, Merlin refused it, instead choosing to wander through the wilderness, drawing on solitude to hone his skills of augury and magic.

Perhaps you already know what became of him many years later? For when mighty King Arthur won the throne of Britain and based his court at Caerleon in Wales, Merlin became his invaluable mentor and adviser. And just as no monarch has ever rivalled King Arthur since that golden age, so there has never again been such a powerful wizard as Merlin.

The Twelve Wild Geese

IRELAND

here were once a king and a queen who ruled over an unusually peaceful realm. They lived in a magnificent palace with every kind of luxury and were blessed with no less than twelve healthy, handsome, strapping sons. But you know how it is: no matter how much some people have, they're never satisfied. So it was with the queen. For she constantly yearned for female company, and the more she thought about the lack of it, the more disgruntled she became.

One winter's day, when the freezing weather had stirred up her peevishness to a frenzy, she stood looking out of her bedchamber window. It so happened that the royal butcher had left a newly slaughtered calf on the snow just below in a puddle of blood, and a raven was standing greedily over it. The queen was mesmerized by the rich colours and, believing she was alone and that no one could hear, she cried out loud: 'Oh, oh, oh! I would give away every single one of my twelve sons if only I could have a daughter with skin as white as that snow, cheeks as red as that blood and hair as black as that raven!'

Then, with a deep sigh, she turned and made ready to go down to the main hall. However, she found her way blocked by a shrunken, deep-eyed old woman she had never seen before.

'I heard your wish, lady,' the old woman hissed at her. 'Even though it's a despicable one, I'll grant you the daughter you long for. But on the very day she's born, the other part will come true as well – and you'll lose all twelve of your sons.'

'Who are you? What are you talking about?' the queen cried in alarm. 'I didn't mean ...'

But the faery woman had already vanished.

*****

The queen told no one what had happened, not even her husband. Within nine months, her belly was heavily swollen with yet another child. To keep her sons safe from the old woman's curse, before she went into confinement she had them all locked up in the strongest room of the palace, with the whole area surrounded by guards. Then, at long last, she gave birth to a beautiful baby girl – with the exquisitely fair complexion, ruddy cheeks and deep black hair she had hoped for. The queen was beside herself with joy and called for the king to come at once and admire their daughter.

There was a long delay before the king arrived, and he was so distraught that he scarcely glanced at the baby.

'Something dreadful has happened!' he told his wife. 'Our twelve boys have all been bewitched! While you were giving birth, the men you'd set to keep them safe suddenly heard a terrible clamour of thunder and whistling. Then they saw our sons transformed, right before their eyes, into huge, grey, wild geese! I was just in time to see them fly like arrows from the window into the sky!'

The queen was even more horrified than he was. For in her heart she secretly knew that the cause of this terrible enchantment was surely the bargain she had so foolishly made in return for a daughter.

Time went by. The king and queen had no more children. Gradually, they came to terms with their tragic loss, especially as their remaining child's beauty was matched by a sweet nature, intelligence and courage.

*****

As the princess grew up, she often wondered why her mother, the queen, was always so troubled. Eventually she discovered that she had twelve older brothers, who had all mysteriously disappeared together, before she could even meet them. Naturally, she wanted to know exactly what had happened. The more she asked, the more the queen's conscience plagued her, until she felt compelled to confide in her daughter.

The princess listened to the confession in horror. However, instead of holding the queen responsible, she blamed herself.

'My brothers would never have been bewitched if I had not been born,' she said, 'so it's my responsibility to rescue them. Don't grieve for them any longer, mother. I shall go out first thing tomorrow in search of my goose brothers, and find a way to return them to their true shapes.'

The queen could not bear to lose her last and best-beloved child, so she did everything possible to prevent the girl from leaving. But it was all in vain. The following night, when the king and queen were fast asleep, the princess bribed some of her guards, slipped past the others and crept through the dark palace garden, through the surrounding woods and out into the world.

She walked a long way through lonely countryside, feasting on wild berries, apples, damsons and nuts as she went. At sunset, she came to a house surrounded by a high hedge. Lamps were shining brightly through the windows, but no one answered her knock. She pushed the door open anyway and went in. A fire was burning brightly on the hearth, the table was laid with twelve plates, knives and spoons, and behind an inner door she saw another room with twelve beds. Then she heard a great rush of wings outside, followed by footsteps, as twelve young men strode in.

Seeing their shock, she immediately apologized for her intrusion.

However, they scarcely heeded her words, for the eldest was exclaiming loudly: 'You fool! You should never have come here – for tonight you must die in revenge for our sorrow!'

The princess stared back at him boldly. 'Revenge? What are you talking about? I have done nothing wrong.'

'Your fault against us is simply that you are a girl,' said a second youth. 'It was on account of a girl's birth that we were all expelled from our father's country, and forced to take the shape of wild geese during daylight hours for the rest of our lives. Because of this, we have jointly sworn an oath to kill the first girl who crosses our path; and in all the years of our bewitchment, you are the first to do so.'

'Then I must be your sister!' she cried. Hastily, she told them what their mother had only just revealed about her brothers' enchantment. 'But I knew nothing of this until yesterday. I promise you, my dear brothers, as soon as I discovered the truth, I embarked on a quest to set you all free.'

The twelve young men looked at each other in consternation. It would be a sin to break the oath they had all sworn so solemnly; yet a far worse sin to murder their innocent sister.

'Whatever should we do?' they lamented.

At once, a low voice called out from the shadows: 'Is it not obvious? Break that wicked oath, which should never have been sworn in the first place!'

Out of nowhere, a shrunken, deep-eyed old faery woman suddenly appeared before them – the very same one who had accosted their mother, the queen so many years earlier. 'Do not lay a hand on your sister,' she said. 'For she is not just your closest kin, but also the only one who can save you.'

The princess, heedless of her royal rank, dropped a humble curtsey before the old woman. 'I desperately want to remove this cruel spell from my brothers,' she cried. 'Can you tell me how to do it?'

'I can indeed,' said the old one. 'But let me warn you, the task you must fulfil is by no means easy. You must go out alone to the moor beyond this cottage, kneel in the bog there and, with your bare hands, gather all the cotton-grass you can find. Bring it back here, spin its silky seed-heads into yarn, weave the yarn into cloth, then sew the cloth into twelve shirts – one for each of your brothers. Once they are all finished, and each of your brothers is wearing one of these cotton-grass shirts, at last the enchantment will be broken.'

'I will go out and begin at once,' the princess said.

But the old woman stayed her with a light hand on her shoulder, saying, 'Wait, my dear, for I have not yet given you the final instruction. This gathering, spinning, weaving and sewing will take you five long years. And throughout that time, you must not speak even a single word, you must not laugh and you must not cry – not even once. For if you break your silence, your efforts will be entirely wasted. Then your brothers will continue turning into wild geese every day until they die.'

*****

The princess went straight out to the moors, tucked up her skirts, waded into the bog and began picking the white cotton-grass that grew there. She worked at her harvest all summer long, until the days grew shorter, darker, wetter and very cold. Then she set up a spinning wheel on which she worked the cotton-grass into yarn, and a loom on which she wove this yarn into cloth. Finally, she took up a needle and sewed the yarn into the first shirt. It was a slow business. When summer came round again, she repeated the whole process from start to finish.

She now lived in the cottage where her goose-brothers spent each night in their human form, but she diligently never spoke a word to them, and certainly never laughed. Despite the misery of her burden, she managed not to cry either. In this way, three years passed, and by the end of that time the eighth shirt was almost completed.

One fine spring morning when she had taken her spinning into the garden, a beautiful greyhound suddenly jumped over the hedge, bounded up to her, laid its paws on her shoulder and gently licked her brow. Behind it, she saw a handsome young man standing at the gate. He asked if he might step in, and she nodded, maintaining her usual silence. He walked up to her, bowed deeply and said, 'My lady, I have often seen you from afar, walking on the moors with your basket of white silk, and longed to make your acquaintance. May I ask your name?'

The princess smiled, keeping her lips sealed.

Despite this, the young man had a great deal to say to her. It turned out that he was a prince from a neighbouring realm, but of course she had no way to tell him that she too was of royal blood. When he asked where she came from and who she lived with, still she was obliged to say nothing.

The prince did not take offence at this, but got down on one knee and said softly, 'My lady, whatever your reasons are for not speaking, I have fallen in love with you. I beg you to marry me.'

At first the girl shook her head vehemently, not wanting to abandon her brothers. But the prince pleaded and begged and reasoned with her, on and on. The more she listened, the more she was impressed by his noble manners, and began to feel very attracted to him. Nevertheless, for the sake of her brothers, she could not marry him unless he let her continue gathering, spinning, weaving and sewing. So she pointed to her spinning wheel, to her basket of yarn and to the pile of shirts she had already completed, with a questioning look.

The prince exclaimed, 'My lady, I understand you wish to continue this splendid work, do you not? Of course you shall, if that is what you desire.'

This promise so reassured her that she nodded eagerly, smiled warmly and put her snow-white hand in his, thus accepting his proposal.

She scribbled a note for her goose-brothers, and propped it up on the table where they were bound to see it when they came home. Then the prince packed her equipment and the finished shirts onto his sturdy horse and lifted her into the saddle behind him. In this way they rode together to his father's palace.

When they arrived, he called a priest and, without fuss or ceremony, the pair were married at once. All the while, the princess maintained her silence. Afterwards, he set up a workroom for her in a quiet part of the

palace, and there she resumed her heavy task. When the days grew longer
and warmer, he showed her a quick way to the moors so she could gather
more cotton-grass; and when the cold nights drew in she returned to
spinning, weaving and sewing.

Nine months after their wedding, in the middle of winter, the princess
gave birth to a baby boy. The young couple were both delighted, but their
happiness was short-lived.

For the prince's father, who was king of that country, had lost his first
wife and married again. The new queen, the prince's stepmother, not
only resented the princess's beauty, but also considered her completely
unsuitable for royal life, what with her constant silence, and working all
day long like a peasant.

So one evening, making sure no one else was around, the wicked
queen gave her daughter-in-law a strong sleeping potion. As soon as it
had taken effect, she snatched the baby from his cradle and hurried to the
window, wondering how to get rid of him without being caught. Gazing
down, she saw a huge wolf pacing restlessly around the grounds, looking
ravenously hungry. So she flung the baby out towards it – and had the
satisfaction of seeing the wolf snatch him up in its jaws at once, before
quickly bounding away. The stepmother now pricked her own fingers
with a sharp needle until they bled, then smeared the blood around the
sleeping princess's mouth. This done, she hastened from the chamber.

When the prince arrived the next morning to see his wife and baby,
he was disturbed to find the cradle empty, and the princess only just

awakening from deep slumber, with dried blood all round her lips. At that moment, his stepmother rushed in, crying, 'Have you seen your wife? She's just killed and gobbled up your poor little son, without even the shame to hide her wickedness!'

At first, the prince could hardly believe that his beloved, gentle, industrious wife could really be guilty of this crime. However, his stepmother flooded him with false evidence and accusations, until he began to change his mind. Nevertheless, he would not let her be publicly accused, so he put out word that the newborn had fallen by accident from his mother's arms at the window, and had then been snatched away by a wild beast.

After this, life in the palace was full of grief, suspicion and sorrow. Nevertheless, the princess continued to gather cotton-grass, to spin it and weave it and sew it, for yet another year, all the while neither talking, laughing nor even crying. This last was more difficult than ever, for she could not mourn properly for her lost son. Sometimes, as she gathered her harvest from the boggy moor, a flock of wild geese would hover overhead; or they would perch on trees in the palace grounds, turning their eyes towards the windows as if trying to peer in. No one but the princess knew they were really her twelve enchanted brothers.

By midwinter, eleven of the cotton-grass shirts were finished, and the twelfth required only the final sleeve to be sewn on before her task was complete. However, she had to delay her work for a second time to give birth, this time to a beautiful baby girl.

Again, she enjoyed only fleeting happiness at this, for the very next day, the prince's stepmother resumed her devilish tricks. Despite the prince's orders that his wife and newborn child must never be left alone, she bribed all the attendants with huge piles of treasure to keep out of the way. Then she again drugged the princess with a strong sleeping potion, snatched the child from her cradle, hurled her outside to be devoured by the same prowling wolf, then smeared blood over the princess's mouth to feign her guilt. Finally, she set up a great screaming, so that the entire palace household came running.

This woke the princess from her drugged stupor, to find herself surrounded by outraged courtiers. All accused her of murder, and urged her execution. Being unable to speak aloud until she had freed her brothers from enchantment, once more she could not defend herself. So she did the only thing she could: seized the last shirt from her work basket, and went back to stitching its sleeve into place.

While she did so, a judge was brought into her chamber. He had words with the courtiers, then declared that the princess must be burned alive that very afternoon, to punish her for the double murder of her own babies. They took her away to be prepared for it, but despite their efforts, could not wrench the twelve shirts from her grasp, including the last one that she was still frantically sewing. Even as they led her to the stake, still she clung to them. She managed to complete the final stitch just before they seized her arms and bound them with tight, coarse rope.

A man now approached, brandishing a taper to light the fire. The princess let the twelve finished shirts fall from her grasp to the ground, and spoke for the very first time in five terrible years, shouting, 'I am innocent!'

The executioners all stepped back in astonishment, for everyone believed her to be completely mute.

The next moment, twelve huge, grey geese appeared from the clouds above and swooped to the ground, right beside the stake. One of these geese used its beak to scoop up a cotton-grass shirt, then flung it over the bird beside him. At once, he transformed into a young man! He then picked up the other eleven shirts, and draped one each over the other geese, which all shapeshifted in the same way. Some of these young men immediately set to work untying the ropes that bound the princess – their sister – to the stake; while the others assailed the executioners with blows that sent them packing.

All this time, the prince had been indoors, unable to bear the misery of watching his beloved wife's execution. When he heard the commotion, he hurried out to find out what was going on – and was overjoyed to see that his wife had been released. He was greatly mystified by the twelve unknown young noblemen with a strong family resemblance who were comforting her. To add to this, another stranger now appeared from nowhere and walked urgently towards the excited group – the shrunken, deep-eyed old faery woman. She was carrying a newborn baby girl, and holding a comely little boy by the hand.

She pressed the baby into the princess's arms, and introduced the awestruck lad to his father, the prince. Then she marched over to the prince's stepmother, who had been watching the unexpected turn of events with undisguised fury. 'What wickedness you have caused!' the faery woman scolded. 'Tossing those poor children away to be devoured by a wolf! Fortunately, that wolf was really me in another shape, and I have taken good care of them both until the time was right to return them to their loving parents.'

With those words, she vanished, and was never seen by any of them ever again.

The wicked stepmother quickly slipped away; but they soon caught her and made sure to give her the ignominious punishment she deserved.

As for the princess, her husband, her children and her twelve beloved brothers: they all lived happily ever after.

The Secret World of the Seals

SCOTLAND

he truth is that some of the seals you find off the coast around here are not ordinary animals, but roane – a noble, shapeshifting race, related to the faeries. Sadly, the only way to recognize one is to kill a seal then watch its carcass. A normal seal just lies there, stone dead. But with a roane, the fur stays vibrant long after the last breath has been knocked from it, bristling up like a pig, then falling back, sleek as a cat; ebbing and flowing until day turns into night and back again with the passing of twenty-four hours.

Not that everyone believes this, of course. Those least likely to are the hunters who kill seals for a living.

*****

There was one such man who lived in a cottage on the seashore near John O'Groats. His tactic for making kills was simple: on sunny days when the seals hauled up on the rocks to bask, he'd creep up behind one with

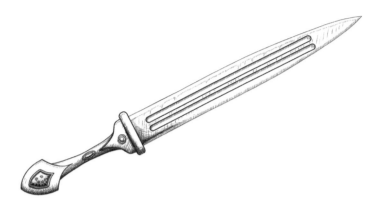

his knife and quickly stab its vital organs. His aim was so true that they always expired at once without a sound. He'd repeat this on one seal after another, then drag them all away and butcher them close by. Sometimes he returned home with half a dozen or more fine sealskins; and from this he made a good living.

But even the most skilled workers have their off-days. It happened that just before sunset one summer's evening, he accidentally missed his target. Instead of killing the seal with a single blow, his knife got stuck awkwardly just under its skin, and he couldn't remove it. The seal gave a blood-chilling shriek of pain, then lurched off the rock into the sea, with the knife shaft still protruding from its back.

The hunter cursed himself loudly for his clumsiness; especially for the loss of his knife, a very fine one which had cost him dearly. He set off for home in a fury. This was worsened when a huge man on an equally huge horse approached him on the road from the opposite direction and stopped right in front of him, completely blocking his way.

The horseman greeted him in a curious, honking voice: 'Good day to you. I wonder if you can help me. I've been told there's a master seal hunter round here, and I'm desperate to get hold of him. You see, I run a fur and leather shop, and I urgently need to fulfil a client's order for a large batch of sealskins.'

When he heard this, the hunter brightened up. 'I'm the very man you're looking for! How many skins do you want, and when do you need them?'

'Ten, at least, by tonight,' said the horseman.

The hunter stood four-square before him, ready to bargain. 'I've got half a dozen in the house you can buy from me at once. For the rest, you'll have to wait until tomorrow, because at this hour all the seals are back in the water. They won't come ashore again until it warms up, well into the morning.'

'Unfortunately, that won't satisfy my client,' said the horseman. 'He wants the full quota of skins this very evening, and all freshly killed – otherwise the whole deal will fall through. And I can tell you, that will be a great loss to you as well as to me, because the payment he's offering is more generous than you can imagine – and I'm willing to split it equally between us.'

The hunter shook his head irritably. 'There's no way to get round this.'

'Oh, but there is,' said the horseman. 'It so happens there's a place along the coast where there are always some seals ashore, even at this late time of day. It's some way from here, so perhaps that's why you don't know it. Get on my horse and I'll take you.'

He gave the hunter a leg-up onto the saddle, then mounted in front of him and shook the reins hard. At once, heading inland, the horse broke into a gallop so fast that the hunter could scarcely keep his seat. On and on they went, while the gathering twilight seemed to turn the grass more vividly green than usual, the pebbles underfoot sharper, and the distant mountains higher. At a desolate spot the hunter had never seen before, they slowed, turned abruptly back towards the sea and stopped on the brink of a high cliff.

'Get down,' said the horseman.

The hunter did so and peered over the edge. 'We'll not find any seals here,' he said. 'There are no flat rocks and no beach for them to lie on. It's a sheer precipice all the way down to the water.'

The horseman grunted and came over to stand beside the hunter. He placed his hand on the hunter's back, then gave him a violent shove – which sent him hurtling over the cliff!

Down and down the hunter fell, past a seemingly endless wall of rigid grey rock. He hit the water with full force, managed to snatch a final deep breath ... And then the waves engulfed him.

Very soon, unable to contain himself any longer, he opened his mouth to gasp and prepared to die by drowning. But to his astonishment, though he was still plummeting through the sea, no water entered his nose or mouth; instead, he was surrounded by fresh air.

Gradually, his descent slowed, until he landed softly on a bed of grey sand. As he came to, he saw the uncanny horseman. He must have dived through the sea after the hunter, and was now standing watching him from a few paces away. Just behind him was an arched door formed from pale coral and studded with shells.

Of its own accord, the door opened. The hunter found himself going through it with an awkward gliding motion as if he were still moving through water. It led into a great chamber with mother-of-pearl walls and a floor of firm yellow sand. It was crowded with figures: not people, but seals.

Strangely, they did not seem surprised to see him. And when he glanced down at himself, he realized why. For by some terrifying enchantment, he himself had transformed into a seal! His legs were too short and his belly too round for him to stand upright, his arms and hands had fused into flippers, his clothes had vanished and he was covered in mottled grey fur.

He gazed fearfully around at the others. They all seemed very mournful, with downturned mouths and tears in their huge round eyes, hissing and honking at each other in subdued voices. They came shuffling closer, completely surrounding him.

Meanwhile, the horseman, still in human shape, had moved away across the sand to another door at the far end of the chamber. He went through it and returned holding a large knife with an ornamented, stag-horn handle. All the seals' eyes were fixed on it. The horsemen held the knife before the hunter's face.

'Do you recognize this?' he said.

It was the hunter's very own knife, the one that he had clumsily lodged into a seal earlier that day, wounding but not killing it.

'Yes,' the hunter admitted. 'It is mine.'

He spoke with humility. For now he understood why the gentle seal people had used magic and trickery to bring him here, and transform him into one of them. They wanted him to understand what appalling crimes he had committed, by repeatedly slaughtering their relations, purely to satisfy his greed for money. Their rightful revenge would surely be to kill him in return.

He gazed around at their solemn faces, longing to fall to his knees, hold up his hands in remorse and beg for mercy. But that was impossible, now he had been cursed into a seal's body. Instead, he could only appeal to them in high-pitched squeals similar to their own: 'I am truly sorry for the harm I've caused to your people! Until you brought me here, I honestly didn't understand the significance of what I was doing. I apologize from the bottom of my heart, and accept that you must punish me in whatever way you see fit.'

He stopped, expecting to hear loud honks and hisses of fury like a human crowd baying for retribution. But instead, there was a long silence as they absorbed his contrite words. Then, one by one, the seals shuffled even closer. He recoiled in terror. However, as each reached him it only rubbed its soft nose and whiskers against his fur, whispering:

'Will you do what we ask ... ask ... ask?'
'Can you help us ... help us ... help us?'
'If you do, we will love you for ever ... ever ... ever ...'

The hunter was truly astonished. How could they not condemn him, after what he had done to them? 'Of course!' he cried. 'Tell me whatever you want, and so long as I'm capable, I'll do it.'

Now the horseman made his way through the circle of seals and lightly touched the hunter's shoulder. At once, he felt a strange shivering sensation and realized he was turning back to his human form.

'Come with me at once,' said the horseman, 'for there is no time to lose.' He led the hunter through the door at the far end.

In the room behind it, a large male seal was lying on a bed of moist green and brown seaweed. His eyes were shut fast and his breathing came in rough, uneven snorts. There was a gaping, bloody hole in his shoulder.

'This is my venerable father,' said the horseman. Before the hunter's eyes, the horseman's own body shimmered and quivered, as he too changed to the shape of a seal. 'Since it is your blunder which left him only half alive this morning, only you have the power to heal him.' He spoke to the hunter as one hurt soul to another. 'I entreat you to do what you can for him.'

The hunter stepped close to the injured seal and crouched by the side of his seaweed bed. 'Sir,' he said respectfully, 'I am deeply sorry for hurting you. I must warn you that I have no medical training, but I know how to cleanse and bandage a wound.'

He turned to the horseman-seal. 'Could you bring me some water? And do you have any clean linen?'

The horseman-seal shuffled off and soon returned with a bowl of salty brine, a cloth and a roll of bandage, all balanced on his head. The hunter knelt by the bedside and gently bathed the old seal's wound over and over with the cloth until it was clean. Then he turned to pick up the bandage; but as he prepared to bind it round the seal's shoulder, something very strange happened. The sides of the wound slowly moved closer to each other and, before his eyes, fused together. Within moments there was no sign that he had ever been injured, apart from a flat scar.

The old seal let out a deep sigh of gratitude. Then he rolled right off the table, shuffled across the floor to a large pool of brine in the corner and plunged into it. When he emerged, shaking off the sparkling drops of water, he was completely cured.

Now the hunter felt himself shift back into his seal shape. The next moment, all the others entered the room and he was caught up in a great wave of seal celebrations. They galumphed towards each other, nuzzling each other's snouts, talking in happy squeals. They took turns to plunge into the sparkling pool and emerge in glistening showers of rainbow-droplets.

They tried to include the hunter as one of them, but he retreated awkwardly to a corner. His head and his heart both felt as if they would explode from the astonishing things he had experienced. Moreover, he was terrified he would have to remain in his seal shape and spend the rest of his life – which was bound to be shortened – living between this underground hall and the open sea.

As the fuss slowly died down, the horseman, also back in human shape, came to him. 'My friend,' he said, now with real warmth in his voice. 'Thank you for saving my father.'

'But I wouldn't have needed to save him if I hadn't injured him in the first place,' the hunter protested.

'That is so,' said the horseman. 'But we roane are a forgiving people. We prefer to remember only the good things that humans do to us, and forget the hurtful ones. I know you feared you were brought here to be punished, but you are wrong. By saving my father, you have cancelled out all your former crimes against us. So I am willing to take you back to your home – on one condition. You must swear a solemn oath never to harm any seal again, whether they be pure animals or shapeshifting roane. For we roane, the seals, and you humans are all kin.'

Although swearing this oath meant he would lose his living, the hunter readily agreed to it. So the horseman gave a loud bellow, summoning all his fellows to gather round and raise a fin in salute. Then the hunter, following the horseman's instructions, held up one hand, placed the other on a shimmering sea scorpion and repeated these solemn words:

I hereby swear
on the ancient laws of the sea
never again to harm any roane or seal
for the rest of my life.

At this, a great cheer of honks and squeals went up. For he had been the most infamous hunter along the whole coast of Scotland, and now they had no further cause to dread him.

'Come,' said the horseman to the hunter. 'Bid farewell to your new friends, for it is time to go home.'

Amidst a flurry of goodbyes and good wishes, he led the hunter out to the grey sand where he had first landed in the underwater country. They linked hands, sprang up in unison and ascended through the sea. Past the surface they soared, through a sunlit morning all the way to the clifftop. Here the horse they had arrived on was patiently waiting. As before, the hunter mounted it behind the horseman and, fast as the wind, they galloped all the way to the gate of the hunter's cottage.

There the hunter – the *former* hunter, we must call him now – reached out to shake the horseman's hand before they parted. But instead of reciprocating, the horseman passed him one of the saddlebags.

'Because of us, you have lost your livelihood,' he said. 'But the roane never take away an honest man's work without giving him fair compensation.'

The former hunter stared at the saddlebag in surprise. 'But what …?'

At that moment, a rush of air and a clatter of hooves made him look up – only to see the horseman galloping away and vanishing round a bend in the road.

The former hunter shrugged, wondering whether this had all been a dream. But the saddlebag felt solid enough in his hand. And when he took it inside his cottage and tipped out its contents on his kitchen table, he found it contained enough gold coins to live on for the rest of his life.

The Most Ancient Creature in the World

WALES

hick was the forest of Gwernabwy. Dappled was the sunlight, and soft the wind that blew through its branches. Like a carpet was its moss floor, tangled with roots, brambles and fallen leaves.

Within these leaves, small creatures scurried, providing daily feasts for Old Eagle and his family. Over countless years, he grew fat and raised his broods on them, generation after generation. Now Old Eagle had so many descendants that he had lost count of them all. Soaring over the spreading trees, roosting on crags with his wife, Eagle Mother, he was completely happy ...

Until one day, as must happen to us all, Eagle Mother died.

Then came the time of mourning with his nine generations of family. Afterwards, they said to him with one voice, 'Old Eagle, you will be lonely if you roost on the crags alone. Take another wife!'

'But I am already related to all the she-eagles in this forest,' said he.

'Then court a bird of a different race,' they said.

'But I am too old and worn to attract a young she-bird of any kind,'

said he. 'Besides, even if I could persuade one to marry me, she would want chicks of her own. I have no strength left to help build a nest, let alone fly backwards and forwards with sustenance while she sat on her eggs.'

'Then find a widow like yourself,' they said. 'One who, like you, is well past breeding and in need of only company and comfort; one at least as old as yourself – or even older.'

Old Eagle saw the wisdom of his family's words, so he made enquiries amongst the other forest creatures. Soon he heard of a bird who many said would be a fine match for him: the Owl of Cwm Cawlyd. 'She is venerable,' folk said, 'far flown, wise, tolerant and compassionate. And she too has lost her mate of many seasons. She would be a perfect second wife.'

So Old Eagle flew alone at dusk to Cwm Cawlyd to spy on the Owl. He concealed himself in a crack in the rocks that overlooked her hunting ground, and waited for her to emerge. Silently out of nowhere, she came, soft and round-faced, wings spread like fans in the twilight. How gracefully she hovered and swooped! How musical was her call, laced with the sadness of bereavement that both had suffered. He saw that she would indeed make him a fine wife, yet still he wavered. For despite what they claimed, Old Eagle feared that she might, in fact, be younger than him. If that were true, she was bound to consider him sluggish and old-fashioned, and would mock his audacious proposal.

So, before approaching her, he decided to make further enquiries.

He called on a friend, the Stag of Rhedynfre, who had been born many winters before Old Eagle hatched from his egg. 'Stag,' said he, 'are you acquainted with the Owl of Cwm Cawlyd? Have you any idea how old she might be?'

The Stag of Rhedynfre pawed up the forest floor with his front hoof and let out a deafening roar. 'Of course I know her! I always have done! Do you see that withered stump of oak tree here by my side? Well, I have lived long enough to remember when it was merely an unripe acorn hanging from a branch. With my own eyes, I saw it fall to earth, sprout its first shoot, develop as a sapling and mature to a majestic tree. Then I saw it tainted by canker which rotted it slowly from the inside until at last, with a creak of agony, it was felled by a storm. I saw woodmen come and chop it up until only this stump was left; then watched it rot away to the remains you see now. This took no less than six hundred years. And even at the beginning of that long time, the Owl of Cwm Cawlyd was already an ancient bird.

'But perhaps you wish to know more about the length of her life? In that case, seek out the Salmon of Llyn Llifon, for she is much older than me. Ask her what she knows of the Owl's history.'

So Old Eagle flew to the river where the Salmon swam, and called down into the water: 'Eminent Salmon of Llyn Llifon! Do you happen to know the age of the Owl of Cwm Cawlyd?'

Nine circles of ripples formed on the surface of the water and slowly faded away. With a splash of silver droplets, the majestic Salmon leaped into the air, spun round, dived back in and began gliding backwards and forwards under Old Eagle's shadow. 'Of course I know the Owl,' she said. 'Look at me, Old Eagle, where I float just below the surface. Can you see all the scales that cover my body? I am sure you could never manage to count them all. Nevertheless, try to guess their number; and add to that the number of eggs that have grown in my roe since first I reached maturity. That total is the number of years that I have been swimming through the waters of this world. I was merely a young fry when first I saw the Owl of Cwm Cawlyd – and even at that time, she was already very old.

'But perhaps you feel you still do not yet know enough about her? In that case, seek out the Blackbird of Cilgwri, for he is much older than me. Ask him what he knows of the Owl's history.'

So Old Eagle spread his wings, flew up and cast his sharp eyes right across the forest, searching in every nook and cranny. At last, he spied the Blackbird of Cilgwri sitting in a clearing on a small piece of grey flint, devouring a worm. He alighted on the grass near the smaller bird, waited for him to finish his meal, then greeted him warmly, asking, 'Honourable Blackbird! Do you know the age of the Owl of Cwm Cawlyd?'

The Blackbird looked guardedly around here and there, thought for a

long moment, then tapped his yellow beak on his seat. 'Look at this flint,'
he said. 'It's so small that one of those vulgar men who sometimes come
stomping through the woods could easily hold it in his hand. Yet I have
lived long enough to remember when the same flint was so huge, it would
have taken three hundred oxen yoked together to move it! It is my own
efforts alone that have worn it away, by striking my wing tip against it when
I awake each morning, and wiping my beak clean on it at night. You can
imagine how many countless years this has taken to reduce it to its present
size. Yet when I was a young chick, the Owl of Cwm Cawlyd was already a
very old lady.

'But perhaps you wish to know even more about her extensive life? In
that case, go in search of the Frog of Cors Fochno, for she is much older
than me. Ask if *she* knows the age of the Owl.'

So Old Eagle flew far beyond the edge of the forest to a place where the
trees gave way to an expanse of grass, dotted with shallow pools of stagnant
water. He flew slowly over it until he spotted a small, greenish-brown
creature with mottled skin and enormous eyes, squatting inconspicuously
in the undergrowth. He landed gently nearby and strutted up to her.
'Distinguished Frog,' he said. Do you happen to know the age of the Owl
of Cwm Cawlyd?'

The Frog blinked at him, carefully considering her answer. At last, she
said, 'When I was a tadpole, the hills that surround this bog did not exist;
this whole land was flat. Since I grew to maturity, I have been slowly eating
the dust here, just a very small amount each day, and it is my droppings
alone that have piled up to form the hills. Think how many years that
has taken! Yet ever since I remember, the Owl you speak of has been
unimaginably old, filling the woods each night with her gentle hooting.
I have outlived most other creatures in the whole world; yet *she* is far more
ancient even than me.'

When he heard these words, at last Old Eagle was satisfied that the
Owl of Cwm Cawlyd was a fitting bride for him. So he went to her roost,
perched on a nearby tree, folded his wings and deferentially asked if she
might marry him. The Owl, who already knew what a glorious bird he was,

was greatly touched and agreed at once. They held a quiet wedding without delay. Since then, they have shared many restful and happy seasons together, greatly enjoying their dotage.

It is only from this story of their courtship that we today still remember the names of the oldest creatures in the world: the Stag of Rhedynfre, the Great Salmon of Llyn Llifon, the Blackbird of Cilgwri and the Frog of Cors Fochno; not to mention the Old Eagle of Gwernabwy himself. But the most ancient creature of them all is, beyond doubt, the wise old Owl of Cwm Cawlyd.

King Cormac
and the Golden Apples

IRELAND

t was a fine May morning. Cormac mac Airt, High King of all Ireland, was walking alone outside his palace on the green hill of Tara, when he saw a man he did not recognize coming towards him. The stranger was a dignified greybeard with the bearing of a warrior, dressed in a gold thread shirt, purple cloak, and shoes of polished bronze. Over his shoulder he carried a curious talisman. It was shaped like an apple tree branch, but its bark was silver and its fruits were gleaming gold.

King Cormac greeted the stranger courteously. 'Who are you?' he enquired, 'and where are you from?'

The greybeard responded to the questions with an enigmatic smile. 'You'll find out who I am when the time is right,' said he. 'As for where I come from, I can only tell you that it is both far away and very different from here. It is called the Land of Promise, because every word spoken there fulfils the promise of truth.'

'Then it sounds far superior to my own wretched, deceitful kingdom,' said King Cormac. 'Tell me more.'

Instead of an answer, the greybeard removed the branch from his shoulder and began waving it slowly about from side to side. In the spring sunlight, its golden apples shimmered. Soft musical sounds drifted from it, reminiscent of a whispering breeze or a baby's gentle breathing. Within moments, Cormac was completely mesmerized. He stumbled onto a nearby bench, laid his sword on the grass and stretched out his limbs with a sigh, as if all the worries of high office were melting away from his heart.

After a while, the greybeard stilled the talisman and put it back over his shoulder.

Cormac rose slowly to his feet, blinking with bewilderment. 'While you waved that branch about, I felt happy and well rested for the first time since I became king,' he exclaimed. 'It must be miraculous.' He lowered his voice. 'Will you sell it to me?'

The greybeard said, 'Sell it? Of course! That's exactly why I brought it here to show you. You have scarcely even glimpsed its full powers. It can heal the sick and wounded, ease the pains of childbirth, soothe distressed minds and soften the withering of old age. In fact it can cure every kind of affliction. Now you know all about it, let us negotiate a fair price for it. How badly do you want it, Cormac?'

Without hesitating, Cormac replied, 'I want it more than anything in the whole world.'

'Are you sure?' the stranger pressed him. 'Do you *really* want it more than anything – or anyone?'

'I have never before desired something so much,' Cormac replied. 'I will pay you generously for it from my most precious treasures.'

'Oh, it's not treasure that I'm after,' said the greybeard. 'This branch can be yours in return for a simple promise.'

'What kind of promise?'

'Only this, Cormac: that you grant me three favours in return.'

'What kind of favours?' asked the king.

The greybeard's answer was evasive. 'Listen, my friend: I'm willing to hand over this branch at once, and not request even the first favour for another full year.'

Cormac was so eager to take the branch that before the greybeard could change his mind, he said, 'This is an excellent bargain. I agree.'

They shook hands and swore a solemn oath on it. Then the greybeard thrust the talisman into King Cormac's hands and vanished into thin air.

Cormac scarcely noticed he was gone, so delighted was he with the golden apples. He carried the shimmering branch straight into his palace, placed it on a table, then summoned all his nobles to admire it. Once they had assembled there, Cormac picked up the branch and shook it slowly about, just as the greybeard had done, quickly filling the hall with its music. At once, everyone began to smile, then to yawn. One by one, they sank onto chairs, stools and even the floor. Cormac himself put the branch back on the table, settled onto his throne and rested his chin on his cupped hand with a grunt of contentment. In this way, the whole court fell into a peaceful, enchanted slumber.

No one woke up until the following morning – when all declared they had never felt so refreshed and at ease. Most invigorated of all was King Cormac himself.

From that time on, the king made it his custom to soothe his court to sleep each evening by waving the branch of golden apples. As the days went by, all who experienced it seemed to grow more youthful and more vigorous. News of it spread across the land, drawing in visitors from far and wide to sample the magic for themselves. Sure enough, it completely cured every malady of both body and mind. As for King Cormac: though well past the flush of youth, the worry lines on his face disappeared, and he became blessed with unquenchable energy.

*****

Thus it went on, day after day, month after month, until a full year had passed.

That evening, as Cormac sat on his throne preparing to wave the golden apples over his court for the coming night, he was interrupted by a

noise outside. The next moment, his guards ushered in the greybeard in his gold shirt, purple cloak and bronze shoes.

'My old friend!' King Cormac cried in delight, 'A hearty welcome to you!'

'Good evening to you too, sir,' said the greybeard sombrely. 'Have you been making good use of the golden apples? Are they as effective as you hoped?'

'I have been, and they are,' the king replied.

'I'm glad to hear that,' said the greybeard. 'Because it's time to pay me the first favour that you promised in return for them.'

'Of course,' said the king. 'Say what you want, and it will be done at once.'

The greybeard bowed, saying, 'Give me Ailbe, your daughter.'

'Did you say ... my *daughter*?' cried King Cormac. The colour drained from his face. 'Oh no, my friend! Ailbe is only an innocent young girl. This is a misunderstanding.'

'It is not,' the greybeard assured him. 'Exactly a year ago, you willingly agreed my price for the apples. It is entirely your own fault that you failed to ask what kind of favours I required. We sealed our bargain with an oath. You cannot break your word by refusing me now.'

'Indeed, I cannot,' said the king. But he looked as if his heart was breaking in two.

Nevertheless, he sent for his daughter. And though all the ladies of Tara shrieked with grief for the loss of her, he allowed the greybeard to take the weeping girl away.

As the palace door closed behind her, one of the nobles nudged the king and reminded him to shake the golden apples over the court. He did so. As soon as the hall filled with their music, Cormac's deep sorrow melted away and he settled down alongside the others to enjoy their usual enchanted sleep.

*****

Another month passed. The greybeard returned to claim the second instalment in the payment of favours. This time, he demanded the king's son, a young boy called Carpre Lifecar. Again Cormac had no choice but to hand him over. And again, the golden apples gave much needed consolation for his loss.

After another month, the greybeard came for the third and final time, saying, 'The last favour I claim from you, Cormac, is your wife, Queen Ethne.'

This was more than King Cormac could endure. For not only did he love his queen dearly, but he greatly feared what would become of her.

But since he had declared that he wanted the golden apples more than anything or anyone, he must let the greybeard take her.

Afterwards, trembling with utter despair, Cormac waved the golden apples wildly about. As always, his courtiers quickly succumbed to slumber. However, this time the magic had no effect on Cormac himself. So in a frenzy of despair, he flung open the palace door and strode into the night to pursue the greybeard.

*****

The king walked and walked and walked, with no idea where he was going. At length he was engulfed by a swirling, unnatural mist. When it finally cleared, he found himself standing alone in an unknown place: a great plain that stretched away in all directions to distant, lowering mountains.

Before him stood a bronze palisade surrounding a silver-walled house. Several men were working on the roof of this house, carelessly attempting to thatch it with white feathers. Suddenly, one called out to the others. They all tossed down their tools and ran off down a winding road in great excitement. After a while they came trudging back, looking embarrassed and despondent. They now tried to resume their work – only to discover that, in their absence, the wind had completely blown away the shoddy section they had previously completed, so that they must start again right from the beginning. Cormac sensed he had witnessed something of significance, but had no idea what it meant. He shrugged and walked on.

Soon he came to another curious sight. A man had started a small fire in the open plain. Unfortunately, the logs he needed to feed it were piled up a great distance away, and were too big and heavy to carry more than one at a time. It took so long to fetch each one that by the time he returned with it, the fire had fizzled out. Thus he had to constantly re-lay and re-kindle it. Because of this, he never managed to enjoy its warmth. Again, Cormac thought this must symbolize something important, but was mystified. So he shook his head and walked on.

At last, he came to a huge, magnificent fortress. Its gates were unguarded and stood wide open, so he walked straight through them onto a wide expanse of grass. On one side of this was a mound, and next to the mound was a well. On top of the well were three big stones, each carved in the shape of a head.

A stream was flowing from the mound into the first stone head, then tumbling out of its mouth. The second stone head had one stream entering its mouth and two streams coming out of it. The third head had two streams gushing into it, but only a bare trickle of water coming out. King Cormac stood and watched them in bewilderment for a while, then walked on.

Just ahead loomed a palace. He walked right up to it and through the open door. A lord and lady stepped forward to greet him, as if they had been expecting him. The lord was tall, sturdily built and grey-bearded, whilst the lady was surely the loveliest ever born since the beginning of time.

'Welcome, Cormac mac Airt!' they said. Then they invited him to sit down and make himself comfortable while he waited.

After a while, a rough-looking man staggered through the door, carrying an enormous pig on his back and an axe in his hand. He dropped the pig onto the floor, swung back the axe, chopped the pig into four pieces and tossed them into a cauldron hanging over the hearth. The fire blazed up under it, making the cauldron of pig flesh bubble and steam.

Cormac's mouth watered, for he was ravenous after his long journey.

However, his host said, 'In order for this pig to be fully cooked, four unlikely true facts must be spoken over it – one truth for each of its quarters.'

'My friend,' said Cormac, 'please demonstrate how this works by telling the first truth yourself.'

'Very well,' said his host. 'Listen carefully. I own seven other pigs like this one – and they alone are sufficient to feed the entire population of this country. For each time one is killed and eaten, I have its bones laid out exactly in place; and overnight it always comes back to life, ready to be slaughtered again.'

'I find that hard to believe,' said Cormac.

The host grinned at him and beckoned him over to peer into the cauldron, while he stirred it with an enormous iron spoon. Sure enough, Cormac saw that one quarter of the pig was now completely cooked through – proving that the host had just told a truth. However, the remaining three pieces were still raw and bloody.

Now the lady spoke up: 'Here is my true fact. The only things I own in all the world are seven cows and seven sheep. Yet these few animals are sufficient to supply all inhabitants here with enough milk to drink, and all the wool needed to weave their clothing.'

'That's impossible,' said Cormac.

'Really?' said the lady. 'Look at the cauldron.'

Sure enough, Cormac saw that another quarter of the pig had confirmed the truth by becoming thoroughly cooked, though the other two pieces remained raw.

It was now the turn of the rough man who had brought in the pig to make his claim. He looked King Cormac directly in the eye, saying, 'You've heard nothing yet, sir. Behind this house there is just a single field. It's never ploughed, never harrowed, never sown with seed and never harvested. Yet in the middle of it stands a small barn, which is kept full to the top with grain all the year round. And though a large quantity is taken from it for milling each day, the amount stored there never goes down.'

Cormac shook his head in amazement, though by now he had learned not to challenge anyone else's truth. So he looked into the cauldron and saw that the third portion of pig was indeed now well cooked, with only one quarter remaining raw.

He returned to his seat and looked at his host frankly. 'I have listened to you with my own ears and seen your miracles with my own eyes,' he said. 'I now realize exactly who you are. You are Manannán, son of the sea god Lir – are you not? – king of this country, which is surely the Land of Promise.'

His host did not deny it.

The lady of the house – Manannán's wife – said to Cormac, 'Now then: we three have all had our turns. So there is only one person left to speak the truth before we can enjoy our feast – and that is you. Tell us what you are doing here.'

'I am travelling through the whole world in search of my beloved daughter, son and wife,' he replied. 'For your husband tricked me to give them away in exchange for a silver branch covered in magic golden apples.'

Manannán nodded, rose from his seat and pointed at the cauldron. 'You told the very truth that I expected you to. Thus the entire pig is now nicely cooked and dripping with rich juice, ready for feasting!'

Cormac followed his hosts to the table and took his seat there. The man who had brought in the pig sat beside him, and opposite them sat Manannán and his wife. Servants piled up their trenchers with pork. But Cormac only looked bleakly at his own helping and made no move to eat.

'Is something troubling you, Cormac?' Manannán's wife asked.

'It is indeed,' he replied. 'It is not my custom to eat with such sparse company.'

'That is quite understandable,' said Manannán. 'But three more people are on their way to join us.'

At that moment, the door opened – and in walked Cormac's daughter, Ailbe, his son, Carpre Lifecar, and his wife Queen Ethne.

They were all overjoyed to be reunited. His wife and children sat down at the table, their plates were filled and everyone began to eat – except for Cormac.

'What ails you now?' asked Manannán.

'I need to ask you some questions,' said Cormac. 'But since you previously tricked me in order to abduct my family, I worry you may not answer them honestly. Now that the pig is fully cooked, what other method is there to ensure you tell the truth?'

'Let me show you my magic cup,' said Manannán.

He snapped his fingers. A servant brought a large golden goblet, richly engraved with mystical patterns, and set it down before him.

'This was made by the finest goldsmith in all the world,' said Manannán. 'Its wonder does not stop at the workmanship. For whenever this cup hears a falsehood spoken, it shatters into tiny pieces. But if it then hears three truths, the fragments join back up together into a perfect whole. Go on, try it yourself.'

He pushed the cup across the table directly in front of Cormac. 'Tell it a lie, my friend.'

Cormac looked at it sceptically. Then he cleared his throat and said with a bitter laugh, 'Ha! I care far more for the golden apples, than for my own wife and children.'

Scarcely had these words left his lips before the golden cup emitted a dreadful creaking noise, cracks appeared across its surface, and it crumbled away to a pile of dust.

'There!' Manannán exclaimed. 'The cup has proved the falsehood of what you just said. Now let me restore it at once by declaring three inviolable truths. Cormac, I swear, firstly, that while your wife and children were in my keeping, they were all well looked after. Secondly, I assure you that none of them were maltreated in any way. Thirdly, I apologize with all my heart for so heartlessly stealing them away from you.'

At once, the gold dust flew up into the air and formed a glittering cloud. Within moments, it had restored itself into the shape of the cup.

Cormac nodded. 'I am very glad to hear that and see that it is true. But Manannán, will you tell me truthfully why you abducted my family?'

Manannán smiled ruefully. 'It was simply an elaborate way to lure you here to the Land of Promise, Cormac, so that we could eat together in friendship.'

'I see,' said Cormac. 'But I have more questions. What is the meaning of the disturbing sights I saw on my journey here? By which I mean: the thatchers whose handiwork was blown away by the wind, the young man whose fire would not stay alight, and the three stone heads of the well, with water flowing in and out of them?'

Manannán replied: 'The thatchers represent people who keep abandoning their work to go on pointless quests to seek quick fortunes – thus never achieving anything in life. The man struggling to keep his fire alight symbolizes those wretched folk who constantly labour for other people, never enjoying the fruits of their own hard work.'

'And what about the stone heads around the well in front of your palace?' asked Cormac.

'Ah,' said Manannán, 'that is the Well of Knowledge. The first head, with one stream flowing into it and a separate one flowing out, symbolizes the person who gives fairly to others in proportion to what he has been blessed to receive. The second head, with one stream flowing into its mouth and two streams coming out of it, represents the admirable person who generously gives more than she gets herself. And the third head, with two streams flowing into its mouth and only a trickle flowing out, is like one who is given plenty but shares very little of it – the most despicable type of person.'

Cormac saw that these statements had not damaged the magic cup at all, indicating that they were all true. 'Manannán,' he said, 'you have just described the whole world's morals, or lack of them. Thank you for sharing such wisdom with me. At last, I am ready to join in with your feast.'

So he ate and drank freely, as did his wife, his children and their hosts. When at last they were all satiated, Manannán's wife led them away to soft beds and spread warm covers over them. They all at once fell into a deep sleep.

*****

Cormac and his family awoke the following morning to find they were no longer in the Land of Promise, but lying side by side on the green in front of the palace at Tara. The magic apple branch and the golden cup had been neatly placed on the grass by their feet.

King Cormac kept these two extraordinary treasures for the rest of his reign. However, on the very night that he died, they vanished, and were never seen again.

The Bogle
of the Murky Well

SCOTLAND

here was once a miller's wife who gave birth to a beautiful baby girl; but on the very night the little one came into this world, she vanished.

How did it happen? No one knew, but what a terrible to-do there was as they all peered into the empty cradle! The mother almost went mad with grief, while the miller blamed everyone he set eyes on.

Then the old grandmother said, 'She's been stolen by the faeries, I'm sure of it. But don't give up hope: they abandon some of the bairns they take if they don't like the look of them. Go and search the woods at once.'

So the miller rushed out. Thankfully, he quickly found the lost newborn in a woodland glade, lying on the crumbling edge of a murky old well. He snatched her into his arms and wrapped her in a warm blanket. But as he turned to carry her back, he stopped short, shivering from head to toe. For an eerie, disembodied voice was drifting out of the trees, chanting:

Remember this time, my honey, my heart,
When we met in the woods down here.
May we both come back to this well one day
And meet once again, my dear.

As the words faded, the little one started to scream. So the miller wrenched himself away, hurried home and gave the baby to his wife. In no time, she was nursing happily, and it turned out that she hadn't been harmed at all.

Days passed; weeks, months and years passed. Memories of that dreadful night were almost forgotten. The baby grew up into a fine young woman, as bold as she was bonny.

*****

But bad luck has a habit of returning. One day, just as dusk was falling, a speckled-brown woodcock flew out of the trees, carrying a glowing tinder in its beak. It headed straight for the mill and set fire to it. In no time at all, the whole building had burned right down to the ground.

To make matters worse, as the miller's family stood staring in dismay at the ruin, a cattle drover came along the road and marched angrily up to them. 'Remember me?' he said to the miller. 'Seven years ago I lent you money to set up your mill, and you promised to pay me back quickly. But you never did – even though I know your business is flourishing. I want that money back – *now*.'

'I don't remember you lending me money,' said the miller in despair. 'And even if you did – can't you see? My mill has just burned down – I've got nothing left, I'm finished!'

'I'll give you a few days,' said the drover ominously. 'If you don't pay up after that, expect trouble.'

The miller and his wife were both tearing out their hair over this double disaster. To get away from them, their daughter went for a walk in the woods, trudging further and further until she reached the glade with its murky well. As she stood staring at it, she suddenly heard an uncanny, rasping voice chanting:

> *I knew you'd come back, my honey, my heart,*
> *Deep in the woods down here,*
> *To meet once again at the well today,*
> *I'm glad to see you, my dear!*

The miller's daughter spun round in alarm. 'Who's there?' she cried.

Twigs crackled and leaves rustled; then a shrivelled little man slunk out from the shadows. He was stained all over with ancient grime, his grin was sly and his eyes were murky as the well itself.

A bogle!

The miller's daughter almost swooned with terror. If only she'd heeded her elders' advice! Hadn't they told her never to walk alone in the woods? Didn't they warn her about this very sinister beastie that lurked in the undergrowth, chanting ditties to turn your bones to ice?

'Oh, please don't come near!' she cried, backing away.

The bogle reached out his cadaverous hands and grabbed her. She struggled hard against him. But he would not let go, and resumed his chanting:

> *I've thought of you often since years ago*
> *We met by the well right here.*
> *I'm so glad to see you again, dear heart!*
> *Come away with me, my dear.*

'No!' the miller's daughter screamed. 'Let me go, you brute! I've never seen you before in my life and I refuse to go anywhere with you!'

But the bogle acted as if he hadn't heard and dragged her into the darkest reaches of the trees. Though he was small, he had the strength of an ox. She fought back with all her might, but could not get free. The bogle reached into a clump of brambles, pulled out a flagon, pushed it

up to her lips and forced her to swallow three gulps of water from it. It was surely bewitched, for at once she fell into a helpless daze. Vaguely, she felt him wrap his arms tightly around her, followed by a rush of wind and a flash of lightning. Were they really rising into the air? Could it be that they were flying? Then everything went blank.

*****

When she woke up, the miller's daughter was lying on a soft couch in the middle of a large, pillared room which seemed to be part of a palace. The furnishings were painted gold and silver, studded with diamonds. Everywhere she looked were diaphanous, long-legged faeries.

A pair of them flitted over to her, pulled her to her feet and led her into a separate room. And who should she see there, sitting on a golden throne? None other than the Faery King and Queen themselves!

'We took you once before, you know, then let you go,' the queen said coldly. 'But this time we intend to keep you.'

The miller's daughter, who knew nothing of her terrible adventure on the night she was born, retorted, 'I'm not staying here. Let me go home.'

The king gave a cruel laugh. 'So you wish to remain in thrall to the bogle, do you?'

'I'm sure I can find a way to be rid of him,' said the miller's daughter.

'You have a high opinion of what you are capable of,' said the queen. 'But it will be amusing to give you a chance and watch you fail. So listen carefully. We'll do as you ask and send you home; but just after you arrive three strangers will come to the door, one by one. You won't like the look of them at all; but even so, you must let each one in. Give porridge to the first stranger, a bannock to the second one and butter to the third – making sure you do this in the right order. But that isn't all.'

She picked up a small green bottle. 'This contains twelve drops of water from the murky well where you met the bogle. Add three drops of it to the porridge, three to the bannock and three to the butter.'

'What about the last three drops of the twelve?' asked the miller's daughter.

'You'll find out when the time comes,' said the king. 'And that will be the hardest challenge of all. Now, begone!'

Before the miller's daughter could ask any more, she was overwhelmed by smothering darkness, and again felt herself flying …

*****

She opened her eyes to see that dawn was breaking. She was standing safely on the doorstep of her own house, next to the burned-out ruin of the mill.

Her parents had been too distracted by their troubles to notice she was missing; they had collapsed into bed at midnight, utterly exhausted, and not yet woken up. So she crept in and made for the stairs; but at that very moment, there came three soft taps at the door, followed by a familiar, blood-chilling voice, chanting:

Open the door wide, my honey, my heart,
Open the door for me here!
Remember how twice we met at the well?
I've come to claim you, my dear!

It could only be the bogle! The miller's daughter was all a-tremble; but nevertheless, she held the door open ...

And saw, not the bogle on the doorstep after all, but a grey-bearded beggar with a menacing look in his eyes. He pushed past her into the house, chanting hoarsely:

I'm starving hungry, my honey, my heart,
So give me some food, my dear.
To honour the times we met at the well,
Pray let me sup with you here.

She longed to run away from him; but, recalling the Faery Queen's instructions, she cooked him a big bowl of porridge, and took care to add exactly three drops of water from the green bottle. The beggar snatched it from her and wolfed it down. No sooner was it all gone, than he vanished.

At once, there came more urgent knocking. This time, it was the angry drover who had ordered her father to pay back his borrowed money. He barged his way in, repeating the beggar's song:

I'm starving hungry, my honey, my heart,
So give me some food, my dear.
To honour the times we met at the well,
Pray let me sup with you here.

What must she give *him*? Ah yes, a bannock. Hastily she prepared the mixture, adding three more drops from the green bottle, then baked it over the griddle. The drover gobbled it ravenously. No sooner was it all gone, than he too vanished.

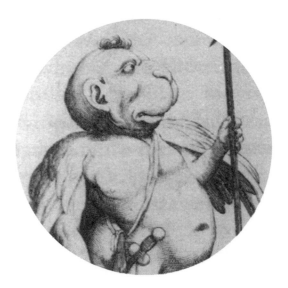

This time, tapping at the door with its beak came the speckled-brown woodcock that had set fire to the mill. It swooped straight in, taking up the drover's song:

I'm starving hungry, my honey, my heart,
So give me some food, my dear.
To honour the times we met at the well,
Pray let me sup with you here.

What now? Ah yes ... The miller's daughter hurried to the pantry, brought out a yellow pat of butter and sprinkled it with three drops from the green bottle. The woodcock perched on the table and pecked it all up greedily. No sooner was it all gone, than the woodcock flapped his wings and vanished ...

And in its place, at last, was the one she had been both expecting and dreading – the evil bogle himself.

Now the bogle took up the song:

> *It's water I want, my honey, my heart,*
> *Give me the water, my dear.*
> *To honour the times we met at the well,*
> *Or I'll die of thirst down here.*

The miller's daughter was now very afraid. For how could the remaining three small drops in the green bottle possibly satisfy him?

'Wait here!' she cried. 'I don't have enough so I'll fetch you some more.'

She grabbed the bottle then ran through the door to the wood, deep into the trees, all the way to the glade and the murky well.

But the bogle had already arrived before her! He spun around her, singing:

> *Don't try to escape, my honey, my heart,*
> *Three drops are enough, my dear.*
> *To honour the time we met long ago,*
> *I'll show you the truth out here.*

He lurched towards her, clutching at the air. She thrust the bottle at him, watching fearfully as he threw back his head and emptied it down his throat.

No sooner was it all gone than he whirled round in a circle and vanished …

… And in his place stood the most handsome and noble-looking young man she had ever seen! Judging by his rich, well-cut velvet clothes and fine leather boots, he must surely be a prince.

The prince bowed deeply to the miller's daughter. 'My dear,' he said, 'at last you see me as I really am. I humbly beg your forgiveness for frightening you so badly so many times in the past. And I thank you with all my heart for being brave and determined enough to save me from my terrible bewitchment.'

'But I don't understand,' said the miller's daughter. 'Who are you? Why do you keep shapeshifting? How can I believe that this is how you really are?'

The prince led her to a fallen tree, bade her sit down, then got down on one knee before her.

'I swear that what I am about to tell you is the honest truth,' he said solemnly. 'I am the son of the King of France.'

'The King of France's son!' she exclaimed.

'That makes me no better than you and no worse,' the prince went on, 'for we have much in common. I was born on exactly the same night as you, and just like you I was snatched away by evil faeries. For a few moments we actually lay together side by side on the edge of the murky well. However, you were luckier than me, because they abandoned you there, where your father found you. But unfortunately, I remained the prisoner of the Faery King and Queen. When I grew up, they transformed me into the hideous bogle you met earlier and replaced my ability to speak normally with those horrible chants you kept hearing. They forced me to torment you and your family in a way that is totally against my nature. But your bravery broke the spells they put on me. Because you successfully completed the challenges they set you, they had no choice but to return me to my true form, and allow me to go home. However, I do not intend to go there immediately, because on the way I hope to marry the bonniest, most admirable lass in all the world.'

'I'm glad to hear I helped you overcome your ordeal, sir,' said the miller's daughter. 'And who is this lass you're planning to marry?'

'Please don't call me "sir",' the prince replied. 'For you are more than my equal – and it's *you* I want to marry. Will you accept me?'

The miller's daughter was astonished. However, she had never before met a man she liked so much, and it didn't take her long to say a joyful 'Yes!'

They went hand in hand together to the miller and his wife and told them everything. You should have heard their exclamations of surprise and delight! By the time they had finished, the sun was high in the sky and

the prince said to the miller, 'If you show me the remains of your mill, sir, I may be able to help you repair it.'

So the miller led the way outside – and was almost as astonished as his daughter had been when she received the prince's marriage proposal. For the mill was no longer a burned-out ruin, but looked just as splendid as on the day it was first built.

While the miller and his wife were hugging each other in relief, there came a rumble of hooves and wheels drawing steadily nearer. A magnificent coach drawn by four pure white horses came round the bend in the road and stopped directly in front of them. Two coachmen in smart livery jumped down and held open the carriage door. The prince handed the miller's daughter inside and climbed in beside her, waving fond farewells to the miller and his wife. And as the coach drove off, he burst into song for the very last time:

Happy at last, my honey, my heart,
So full of rapture and cheer.
Evil enchantment replaced by love.
For ever after, my dear!

The Sleeping King

WALES

here was once a youth who was the seventh son of a seventh son – which meant he was blessed with uncanny luck. One evening in the village inn, he met a man who told him that the streets of London were paved with gold, adding, 'A lucky lad such as you is bound to make your fortune there.'

So the youth packed his bags and set off for London. He hadn't gone far before he spotted the most enormous old hazel tree he had ever seen growing by the roadside. He cut off one of its straight, springy stems to fashion himself a walking pole, and with this strode all the way from south Wales to London in less than ten days.

However, when he arrived, he was disappointed to find that the capital of England was in fact an overcrowded, dirty place with not a single piece of gold in sight. Nevertheless, knowing that success never comes without effort, he made his way through the city, speaking cheerfully to all the Londoners he met, hoping someone might point him in the direction of easy pickings. Standing on London Bridge, he fell into conversation

with an elderly man whose long, dark robe and curious, cone-shaped hat indicated he was a wizard.

The wizard looked him up and down from head to toe, then said in a low, hoarse voice, 'You're looking to get rich, lad – am I right?'

The youth nodded.

'Well, that's not going to happen here in London. You need to go back to where you came from.'

'Back home?' said the youth. 'No one could ever get rich in that godforsaken hole.'

'Not quite all the way to your home,' said the wizard. 'Just as far back to the place where you cut that fine hazel staff you're carrying. Haven't you noticed the curious patterns in its bark? They didn't get there by accident, you know. They're a sure indication of vast treasure hidden under the roots of that tree.'

The youth stared back at the wizard sceptically, but nothing in the old man's demeanour gave reason to doubt his word.

'So ... How do I find this treasure?' he asked.

The wizard put a gnarled hand on his arm. 'You won't find it unaided. And even if you did, you couldn't take it out by yourself without being fatally attacked in the process. But if you show me where this hazel tree grows, I'll help you.'

The youth hesitated. But at that moment, a carriage rolled by, spattering mud all over his clothes, which were already covered in soot and dust. So he said, 'All right. I've had enough of this filthy city. I'll show you the way, sir – if you'll show me this treasure.'

*****

They walked all the way back to south Wales together, though the wizard was poor company and made no conversation at all. However, that changed as soon as they reached the hazel tree from which the youth had cut the walking pole.

'Dig down here at once!' the wizard cried, reaching into his robe.

From somewhere in its folds he drew out a spade. How on earth had he managed to conceal such a large tool throughout their journey? No matter, he thrust it into the youth's hands, saying, 'Quickly, don't waste time!'

So the youth set to work, while the wizard urged him on: 'Further, deeper! Don't give up, you're almost there!'

At last, he uncovered a very large stone slab.

'Lift it!' the wizard cried.

The youth eased the spade under the edge and, with great effort, managed to heave the slab out of the way. He expected to find a treasure chest buried directly beneath it; but instead there was just a gaping hole, from which steep stone steps led down into darkness.

'What are you waiting for?' the wizard said impatiently. 'Go down there at once. I'll come directly behind and, when we reach the bottom, I'll guide you.'

The youth took a last breath of fresh air and gingerly descended the steps. Finally, he reached the bottom, where the wizard joined him. Just enough light shone through the opening above to reveal the entrance to a passage ahead, with something gleaming brightly halfway along it.

'We go down here,' said the wizard, pointing. 'But listen carefully and take great care. This passage is partly blocked by a bell hanging from the ceiling. Whatever you do, don't touch it – or we'll be in trouble.'

The youth nodded and followed the wizard towards the bell. The radiance came from its shell of burnished bronze, cast into the rounded shape of a beehive. They both got down onto hands and knees to pass underneath it.

Shortly afterwards, the passage opened up into an enormous cavern, and the youth stopped short in utter astonishment.

For this place was lit by another radiance. It came from countless highly polished swords, shields, spears, knives and battle-axes, strewn all over the floor; and also from gleaming suits of armour encasing the bodies of hundreds of warriors, lying on their backs in concentric circles amongst the weapons. By the steady rising and falling of their chests it could be seen they were not dead, but merely sleeping. The brightest light came from the most impressive warrior of all, who wore a heavy golden crown on his head. He was sitting upright on a splendid throne at the far end of the cavern, though he too was fast asleep.

'Who are they?' the youth whispered.

'Surely you can guess the name of the man on the throne?' the wizard replied. 'Don't you recognize the sword he is holding?'

The youth stared at him blankly.

'The sword is Excalibur,' said the wizard. 'This is none other than mighty King Arthur himself! The men spread around him on the floor are the Knights of the Round Table.'

'King Arthur and his knights?' The youth could hardly contain himself. 'But surely they all died in battle hundreds of years ago?'

'Keep your voice down!' hissed the wizard. 'Have you not studied history? King Arthur and his knights did not die, but were taken across the sea to the mystical isle of Avalon, where their wounds were healed by nine queens of faery magic. Afterwards, they were sent back here to sleep safely inside this cavern, deep below the earth.'

'Forever?' whispered the youth.

'Nothing is forever,' said the wizard. 'A time will come when the hawk and the eagle will again go to war, putting the island of Britain into mortal danger. Then the bell we just passed will ring to waken them, and King Arthur, restored to glory, will lead out his knights to save our land. But they will not need their treasure for this, so you may help yourself to it. Come.'

He took the youth around the sleeping warriors and past King Arthur on his throne. None of the men stirred. They crept behind the throne, through an open door into a low-ceilinged storeroom. Here the youth saw two great piles of coins and other treasures, one of silver and one of gold.

'You may take as much as you want from either of these piles,' said the wizard. 'But whichever pile you choose, be sure not to touch the other.'

The youth stumbled straight to the pile of gold. With great excitement, he began cramming coins from it as fast as he could into his pockets and under his shirt. When there was no space for any more, he seized an enormous golden goblet and wrapped his arms around it.

'Are you done?' the wizard asked.

The youth nodded. 'But what about you, sir? Aren't you taking anything?'

The wizard's eyes glimmered like pools in the unearthly light. 'What do I want with treasure? The only things I yearn for are more knowledge and wisdom. Now then, I'll lead you back to the steps. Remember to take great care as we pass the bell along the passage. Whatever you do, don't touch it!'

'I won't,' the youth assured him. This time, when they reached the bell, he got down flat right onto his belly to wriggle underneath it. But in doing so, he had to hold the golden cup aloft; and, despite his best efforts, it slightly scraped the bottom of the clapper.

At once, a sonorous noise rang out right along the passage and into the chamber.

The youth froze, then made to hasten away. But it was too late.

For a deep male voice suddenly boomed, 'The bell has rung! The day has come! My lord King Arthur, awake!'

The hundreds of warriors sleeping in the cavern began to groan and stir.

The wizard spun round, his dark cloak awhirl. He called into the chamber, 'No, no! Good knights, the bell was rung in error. The day of your rising is still many years away. Lie down, my friends, sleep on!'

The musty air filled with sighs. Gradually, very slowly, the noises died and the movement stopped until the cavern was again as still and silent as a grave.

The wizard now ducked under the bell, hurried after the youth and helped him back up the steps. At the top, he told the youth to shift the stone slab back into place, and cover it again with soil and turf. Soon there was no sign of any disturbance under the great hazel tree.

'So,' said the wizard. 'You found the fortune you longed for so much, and now it is time for us to part. We will not meet again. If you look after your gold carefully, you will live your whole life in comfort.'

'But supposing it isn't enough?' said the youth. 'Supposing I have an

accident or some other disaster, and I can't help using it all up? May I go back and fetch more?'

'If you have to, you must,' said the wizard brusquely. 'But remember what you learned today. Do not touch more than one pile of treasure, and take the greatest care not to strike the bell as you pass it. If, inadvertently, you do strike it again, repeat the words you heard me say to send the warriors back to sleep. Now, farewell!'

The youth reached out to shake his hand in thanks. But he gripped only empty air, for the wizard had already vanished.

*****

The youth carried his treasure home, stored it carefully in a secret hiding place under his bed and tried to spend it both thriftily and sensibly. Despite this, before long he had squandered the entire amount.

So he went back to the hazel tree, found the spot where he had dug before, shifted away the stone slab and went down the steps, back into the cavern. Everything was exactly as they had left it: still and quiet but for the low sound of the sleeping warriors' breathing. This time, when he crept round to the storeroom, he helped himself to a hoard of silver, not touching the gold. When he carried his hoard down the passage, he took utmost care not to touch the bell. However, despite his best efforts, again he could not prevent the edge of a huge goblet brushing against the clapper. Cringing, he heard the sonorous clangs resounding across the cavern, followed by drowsy voices calling, 'Has the day really come this time? Is the battle upon us? Must we wake King Arthur?'

'No, no, no!' the youth shouted back at them. 'Not yet. All is peaceful. Sleep on!'

'On whose authority do you tell us this?' they hissed.

The youth thought quickly and answered, 'I am the spokesman of the wizard.'

'The wizard?' they called back to him. 'Do you claim to speak for *him*?'

The youth swallowed and said, 'Yes indeed. He commands me to tell you: sleep on!'

Just as last time, the voices died down until all was peaceful and still. The youth fled as fast as he could, carrying the silver with him.

*****

If only he had learned his lesson! But instead, surviving those two adventures turned him into a reckless fool. He spent the silver he had taken from the cavern intemperately, so that very quickly it too was all used up. *That doesn't matter*, he thought. *I can easily get some more.*

So he went back to the hazel tree and dug down for a third time, uncovered the stone slab and hastened down the steep steps into the cavern. This time, he ducked under the bell so carelessly that it clanged while he was still on his way in.

At once, the warriors all began calling out.

He answered them brazenly, 'It's not your time yet, knights, sleep on!' and hurried past them into the storeroom. This time, he seized coins from both the gold and the silver piles.

But he had scarcely even half-filled his pockets, before he heard heavy footsteps behind. A huge hand thumped down onto his shoulder. His assailant spun him round and jerked back his head, forcing him to look up into the fiery eyes of a knight, at least two full heads taller than he was.

'Get out, you liar, you thief and swindler!' the knight roared at him. 'Never dare enter King Arthur's treasure house again!'

He lifted the youth from his feet and dragged him, like a dead rat, back past the throne and the other warriors – who were all wide awake now, and working themselves into a battle rage. He hurled the youth up the steps. On the way, all the coins he had stolen that day came tumbling out of his pockets. When he reached the top, the youth scrambled out in terror, slid the slab back into place, covered it with turf and fled.

As he ran, he glanced back over his shoulder. But the old hazel tree was no longer there – not a single trunk, stem or even root of it.

Though the youth tried many times afterwards to return to that place, he never found it. And sad to say, because he had abused the luck granted as birthright to a seventh son of a seventh son, he spent the rest of his life in poverty.

The Merrows' Song

IRELAND

fisherman once abandoned common sense and went out to sea when a fierce storm was blowing up. The result of this foolhardiness was that he never came home.

The fisherman left behind a wife, an old mother, an infant daughter and a young but courageous son. Eonín, the lad was called. When Eonín heard his mother and grandmother keening, and the baby wailing, he knew without being told that something terrible had happened to his father. He thought to himself, 'As I'm the only man in the house now, I'd best do something about it.' So, although night was now falling, he sneaked outside, climbed over the stone wall into the lane and ran through the gale to the beach.

He had a plan. He had often heard it said that fish-tailed merrow women lurked in the water below the rocks at the far end of the sand, waiting to drag the unwary away to a watery death. And he knew that was true, because on stormy days like this one, he had often stopped to hear their eerie songs drifting up from the deeps – even though he'd been warned that the merrows abhor eavesdroppers and punish them severely.

His father's disappearance must surely be linked to this. So he would wait there until a merrow made her presence known. Then he would get down on his knees, apologize for his indiscretion, and beg her to send his father safely home.

By the time he reached the rocks it was completely dark, but he knew them well enough to feel his way nimbly across. Below, the sea was still choppy and wild. As he reached the furthest point, a great wave suddenly swept right over him, knocking him to his knees. He tried to cling to the seaweed draping the rocks, but it was too slimy for his desperate fingers. In this way, the sea took him into its treacherous embrace.

He sank down and down, holding his breath until he could no longer do so. To his relief, instead of choking, he found that even in the water he could breathe quite normally. Further and further he sank ... and landed softly, not on rock or sand, but on something soft, warm, elongated and writhing – a living creature.

A hoarse voice called out, 'Get off me, you wretch!'

The creature was longer than Eonín was tall, slightly fatter than a snake, with a dull grey body and a pale belly. Instead of limbs it had two short, feathery protrusions just below its head, and a long, feathery ridge right along its back. Its eyes were like round, black beads circled by shimmering rings, and its grinning mouth was spiked with teeth. It was a huge conger eel!

Congers are almost as dangerous as merrows, so Eonín knew he must play his cards carefully, to get the upper hand. 'Apologies if I hurt you, Mr Conger,' he said. 'But I've just suffered a terrible accident!'

'Accident, eh?' the conger replied. 'In that case ... Hmm, I suppose you deserve sympathy. Well now, you seem to know my name – so what's yours?'

'I'm Eonín, son of Séan Costello the fisherman,' said he.

The conger gave a great lurch, tossing Eonín off his back, onto the gritty sand that surrounded them. 'Séan Costello? What an extraordinary coincidence!' it exclaimed. 'I once met your father, lad, years and years ago ... And now here you are, appearing out of nowhere and jumping all over me! I was only a young elver at the time, shorter than your own arm. I got caught in your father's net, and thought for sure that my end had come. But instead of cutting me up for bait, he untangled me and tossed me back into the sea. "It's not fair to catch a small fry like you," he said. I've never heard such decent words, before or since, and never forgotten them. I often used to spy him out in his boat after that, and always did what I could to ease his passage. Remember me to him when you get home, lad. Tell him I'm now ten feet long with jaws strong enough to bite right through his hand ... Not that I ever would, seeing how he spared my life.'

Eonín said, 'I can't pass on your message, Mr Conger, because my father's gone missing at sea. I was hoping for a chance to ask the merrows if they'd taken him and, if so, beg them to send him home. But while I was searching for them, the sea surged up and swept me down here.'

'Merrows?' The conger spat out the word. 'Those interfering, callous creatures? I strongly advise you to keep right away from them.'

'I can't sir,' said Eonín. 'I badly need their help to get my father back.

Have you any idea where I could find them?'

'Hmm,' said the conger. 'In return for your father's good deed, I suppose I'm obliged to take you to their cave. But I'm not going close to them; I'll drop you off nearby.' He lay flat, folding down the great fin that ran along his back from head to tail. 'Stretch out on top of me, put your arms round my neck and cling on tight.'

As soon as the lad was settled, the conger shot off like an arrow from its bow and swam swiftly through the depths. At length, he came to rest on a different expanse of sand, this one pure white, scattered with glimmering shells and brightly coloured seaweed, guarded by towering cliffs at either end. Eonín jumped to his feet and gazed around.

'Listen,' said the conger. 'Can you hear them?'

Drifting from a dark cavity in one of the rock faces came the sound of women's voices, sweet as honey, yet bitter as abandonment.

'They're in there,' said the conger ominously. 'You'd best be bold when you go in, get straight to the point and tell them exactly what you want. They're bound to try distracting you with both threats and temptations; but ignore that and insist they take you to their queen. She's the one you need to appeal to. Good luck!' With that, he shot away up through the water.

The lad followed the singing through a rough archway in the cliff. Soon he found himself in an enormous cavern, softly lit by a shimmering floor of sand, topped by a roof of thatched seaweed. The cavern was crowded with merrow women. They stood motionless, their exquisite, expressionless faces framed by long green hair, their fish-tails a swaying dazzle of silver, heads thrown back as they sang.

One by one they saw him, fell silent and turned to stare. Then they came drifting towards him, holding out their hands enticingly, chanting, 'Welcome, stranger! Stay with us awhile and share our songs! Dance with us and be happy!'

But Eonín shook his head and demanded, 'Where is your queen?'

They pointed to the rear of the cavern. Seated on a great rock there, he saw a lone merrow who outshone the others just as the moon transcends

the stars. She beckoned to him, calling, 'Who are you, stranger? What do you want of us?'

He found himself involuntarily drawn towards her, like a young dog on a leash. But when they were standing face to face, he met her cold gaze steadily and said, 'My name is Eonín Costello. I've come to claim my father, Séan.'

The queen did not deny that they had taken Séan. 'Do you now?' she said. 'Well, perhaps you're not aware that here in Undersea, we do not grant wishes just for the asking. However, we do sometimes strike bargains with mortals, though few are willing to agree the terms we set. So here's my offer: I will release Séan to go home – if *you* will stay here in his place.'

Naturally, the lad was shocked. But after considering it for a moment, he said, 'I have no choice, do I? My mother and grandmother are both wasting away with grief for him, and neglecting my baby sister. I'm not strong enough yet to take out my father's fishing boat, so without his earnings, they'll all starve.'

'Are you sure?' she taunted him. 'Do you really want to give up your life so young?'

Eonín said falteringly, 'Yes. I am sure.'

Barely had he spoken these words before the merrow queen was pressing her hand against his heart. A great chill overwhelmed his body. And with that, he immediately forgot everything: his old life, his family, even his reason for entering the strange world of Undersea.

*****

Time passed. Day and night were distinguished only by the green air getting lighter and darker. Eonín now lived alongside the merrows, swimming with them, sharing their work of keeping the sea-ways clear for passing fish and other marine creatures. But he was excluded from their most important job: the clearing of dead bodies from shipwrecks after violent storms.

On one such occasion, loitering alone outside the cave, the conger eel came swimming by.

'So we meet again,' he smirked. 'I guessed we would. No doubt they refused to let you have your father back, eh?'

'Father?' said the lad in bewilderment, for his memory was a total blank. 'What is a father? And who are you? You speak as if we already know each other; but I've never met you before.'

'They've bewitched you!' cried the conger in disgust. 'Ach, those scheming merrows have got you totally in their power. Well, while they are busy elsewhere, I shall take the opportunity to release you.'

'Bewitched?' said Eonín. 'Power?'

'Enough!' exclaimed the conger. 'Wait here.'

He shot off through the water. Within moments he was back, thrusting a wad of reddish-brown seaweed at Eonín. 'Eat this!' he commanded.

The lad had no desire to eat it, but nor did it repel him; he was now simply indifferent to everything. Obediently, he took a bite – and at once its salty crispness brought back a memory. Dried dulse seaweed, the treat his mother used to give him! With that single taste, everything he had forgotten flooded back into his head: the cottage where he lived, the beloved family who shared it with him, the fields around it with their stone walls, and his father's boat bobbing on the dappled water beside the quay. And with those memories came a great sorrow.

'What's going on?' he cried.

'Since you vanished,' said the conger, 'your people have been constantly searching for you in the sea around your village – at the water's edge and out in boats, with your father leading them ...'

'My father? But I remember now: he drowned!'

'No,' said the conger. 'He got his life back – presumably thanks to you. But your people don't know that you came here voluntarily. They reckon you were washed away and they're desperately trying to find your body. Your mother and grandmother are distraught, your baby sister won't stop crying, and your father's not spoken a word since he discovered you were gone. But it's not just your people who are suffering – it's all us sea creatures too. Because the search parties are using heavy poles and sharp grappling irons, stirring up the water, damaging the seaweed and terrifying us all. Unless they stop, we'll all have to abandon the islands, even the fish. Then the whole sea will become lifeless and the fishermen will never get another catch.'

Eonín gathered his thoughts together. 'I must go home at once, to see my family and save the sea creatures,' he said. 'But I can't, Mr Conger. You see, just before I lost my mind, I struck a solemn bargain with the merrow queen. I promised to stay here forever, in return for my father going free.'

The conger said, 'All is not lost. We'll go and seek help from the wise Great Grey Seal of Skerdmore. Come on: I'll take you to him at once.'

Again, he flattened the fin along his back, Eonín lay along the conger's body, and they shot off through the water.

Eventually, they emerged above the surface by a small, craggy island where an enormous grey seal was resting. The conger hooked his tail round a rock, enabling Eonín to scramble ashore. Then he addressed the seal with great humility and respect saying, 'Your eminence, forgive us for intruding on you. We have come to request the benefit of your wisdom and learning to help us solve a difficult problem. This young man sacrificed his life to the merrows, in exchange for them releasing his father, who they had taken for their own sinister business. However, he now urgently needs to break the bargain he made with them, so he can return home.'

The Great Grey Seal peered at Eonín intently. He said, 'I often have dealings with the merrows, for we are distant kin. Perhaps you have heard me singing with them on warm summer nights?'

'I have indeed,' said the conger. 'In my humble opinion, your eminence, your voice is far superior to theirs.'

The Great Grey Seal opened his whiskery mouth in a broad smile. 'Thank you, Conger. In return for your flattery, I will help your human friend.' He wriggled heavily over the rocks until he was close enough for the lad to catch his musky scent. 'Listen, young man. The merrow queen may be persuaded to let you go if you give her what her heart most desires.'

With those words, he slid into the water with a loud splash and swam away.

'But how can I find out what the merrow queen desires?' cried Eonín in despair.

The conger said, 'It's a common failing of humans to make difficulties where none exist. All you need do is ask her.'

He ordered the lad to lie on him again, and carried him back the way they had come.

The merrows had returned to the cavern before them, and were filling
the air with their habitual eerie singing. Their queen beckoned Eonín
over, saying, 'Where have you been hiding? I can see in your eyes that
something has happened to make you change. Speak!'

'My memory has returned,' he admitted. 'Also, I have discovered that
I'm urgently needed at home; and that you will release me if I give you
your heart's desire. Tell me what that is.'

The queen laughed coldly. 'My heart's desire? It is merely a song.'

'You're making fun of me,' said Eonín. 'The merrows already have all
the songs in the world.'

'So you think,' said she. 'Oh, we do indeed have plenty of songs: merry
and cruel, tragic and haunting. But none are good enough for the strange
new thing that has unexpectedly appeared in our midst. Give me a song
that no merrow has ever sung or even heard before. If it is good enough, I
will indeed release you.'

The lad closed his eyes and thought for a long time – of sea shanties
and rope-pulling chants; songs for when nets are dropped, and for when
they are hauled up again; verses to greet laden fishing boats returning to
harbour after long hours out at sea. But these were always sung aloud and
out of doors, so surely the merrows had already heard them.

Then his thoughts turned to his mother, who hated the sea; and to his
infant sister, too young to even know what it was. And there came into his
head the lullaby that his mother used inside the cottage, to send his sister
to sleep. He began to whisper it under his breath.

The queen listened intently, then seized his arm, saying, 'Come this
way.'

She led him into a dark recess of the cavern and down a passage
towards an ugly grizzling sound. At the far end was a small driftwood
cradle lined with sea-moss. On it lay a tiny baby with a silvery fish-tail,
tossing and turning miserably, mouth twisted into a scowl.

'Sing the same song again,' ordered the queen.

As he did so, she added curious melodies of her own, so that they were
singing it in harmony, over and over. Gradually, the merrow baby calmed,

gurgled and began to smile.

The queen said, 'Your song has done what we considered impossible. For this, I will gladly release you.'

She reached out and put her hand over his heart, exactly as before. This time, however, instead of chill, the warmth of life gushed into his body, spreading down his limbs to his fingertips and toes. He felt faint and light-headed.

Vaguely, he was aware of the merrows leading him back through the cavern to the white sand outside it. Dimly, he saw the conger eel awaiting him. Shakily, he clambered onto its back, put his arms round its neck and felt it rise through the water.

They emerged by the rocky outcrop at the end of the beach below his cottage. He slipped off the conger's back and stepped onto dry land for the first time in many months.

'Farewell, my friend,' said the conger. 'Remember me to your father.' Then he slipped quickly into the water like a long shadow, and melted away.

The sun was rising into a clear, early-morning sky. Eonín stood on the rocks, slowly drinking in the familiar scene; and as he did, the memories of his time in Undersea faded away like the last breaths of a dying wind. He saw a boat laden with fish making its way to the harbour, with his father standing in the bows. As they waved at each other, he heard a woman shouting, 'Eonín! So there you are! Whatever's dragged you out of bed so early?' His mother, babe in arms, came hurrying down the path, with his grandmother tottering behind her.

And by that time, his entire adventure was already forgotten.

The Black Bull of Norroway

SCOTLAND

ar across the sea in Norway – or Norroway as the old folk used to call it – there once lived a lady who had three valiant daughters.

One day the eldest daughter said, 'Mother, give me a bannock and a slice of roast meat, for I'm off to seek my fortune.'

With these, the girl walked out into the morning. On and on she went, until she reached the cottage of a kindly old witch. The girl greeted her politely, and asked advice for her quest.

'Well now,' said the witch, 'I may be able to help you. Step inside, then look out through my window until you see whatever it is that you're seeking.'

The girl thanked her, went into the witch's cottage and did as she suggested. She saw nothing of interest on the first day, and nothing on the second. However, on the third day she saw a grand coach and six horses coming down the road.

'That's for you!' said the witch. 'Hurry outside and show yourself.'

So the girl did. The coach slowed down and stopped before her. Someone inside opened the door and beckoned, so the girl climbed in; and that was the last anyone ever saw or heard of her.

A very similar thing happened with the second daughter. She also asked her mother for a bannock and a slice of meat so she could set out to seek her fortune, walked to the witch's house, was invited inside and advised to watch from the window. She saw nothing much on the first two days, but on the third day a slightly less grand coach, with only four horses, came along. Well, that was good enough for her, so she went outside and got into it; and she too was never seen or heard of again.

Then it was the turn of the third and youngest girl. You can imagine how sad her mother was to see her very last daughter set off down the road, with only a bannock and slice of meat to sustain her as she travelled to goodness knows where. This girl too accepted the witch's invitation to enter the cottage and watch from the window. Like her sisters, she saw nothing of interest on either the first or second days. On the third day, no coach and horses came for her; only an enormous bull covered from nose to tail in pure black hair.

The girl was petrified with terror at the size of him and the sharpness of his horns. But the old witch said, 'This one's for you. Be brave and remember: some things are not what they seem.' She took the girl by the hand, led her outside and told her to climb onto the Black Bull's back. When the girl refused, the witch lifted her up there herself; and at once the Black Bull walked away with her.

They had not gone far before the Black Bull turned his head and said over his shoulder in a soft, crooning voice: 'Welcome, my dear. I do hope we'll be friends, because we have a long way to travel together. No doubt you'll soon feel hungry and thirsty. All you have to do is reach your hand into my right ear to find some nourishing food, and into my left ear whenever you need to drink. I have more than enough to keep you satisfied, so help yourself to as much as you wish.'

Well, that was better than she had expected! The Black Bull carried the girl so gently that she started to enjoy her ride, especially when she found that the food and drink he spoke of was both easy to take and delicious to taste. Thus their shared journey passed very quickly, and when sunset streaked the sky with red and gold, they came to a splendid castle.

'This belongs to my eldest brother,' said the Black Bull. 'We're staying here tonight.'

They passed through the gates to the door, where servants helped the girl to the ground and ushered her inside to sleep, while the Black Bull grazed in the pasture.

The next morning, a maid showed the girl into the parlour and put a red apple into her hand, saying, 'Take care of this until a day when you find yourself in despair. Then break it open, and use what's inside to help you.'

The girl thanked her, put the apple into a small bag hanging from her belt and went outside. Her friend the Black Bull was already there waiting for her, and this time she clambered onto his back with great eagerness. They continued their journey together until twilight, when they stopped at an even more splendid castle.

'This belongs to my second brother,' the Black Bull told her. 'We're staying here tonight.'

Again, she went indoors to sleep while the Black Bull grazed in the meadows. The next morning, a maid took the girl into the parlour and put a yellow pear into her hand, saying, 'Keep this until your despair gets worse. Then break it open and use what's inside to help you.'

The girl thanked her, put the pear alongside the apple in her bag, and went outside to find the Black Bull, who she greeted with great affection. Thus they travelled on, until at nightfall they reached the most splendid castle of all.

'This belongs to my third brother,' the Black Bull told her. 'We're staying here tonight.'

As before, she slept inside the castle while the Black Bull made himself at home in the fields. The next morning, she was taken into another parlour and given a purple plum by a maid who said, 'Keep this until you are in the deepest despair of all. Then break it open, for what's inside may finally save you.'

The girl thanked her, put the plum alongside the apple and pear in her bag, and went out to the Black Bull. This time, however, their journey was different. For instead of travelling to another castle, when darkness fell they stopped in a desolate, gloomy valley surrounded by ominous mountains. There the Black Bull told the girl to get down.

'Surely we're not spending the night here?' she asked him.

'I'm afraid *you* are,' said the Black Bull, sounding troubled. 'You see, you must wait here while I carry out an important task: I have to fight the Devil.'

'The Devil!' she cried in horror. 'But why?'

The Black Bull only shook his head sadly and said, 'Now then, there's something important you must do to ensure my victory. Until I return, sit absolutely still here on this boulder. Do not move at all, not even a single hand or foot.'

'I promise to do that,' she said. 'But how long must I wait for you?'

'Not long once the battle is over,' said the Black Bull. 'And you will know when that time comes, because the air will change colour. If it turns red, the Devil will have beaten me. But if it turns blue – as I hope it will – you will know that *I* have won. Remember: *Do not move until I return!*'

She sat down on the boulder and made herself comfortable. Then he galloped off and quickly vanished into the gloom.

The girl waited on and on, hearing nothing and seeing nothing. At last, the air around her began to turn vivid blue. Thus she knew that the Black Bull had won the battle. Naturally, she was overjoyed; not just because she hated waiting alone in the gloomy valley; but also because she had grown to love the Black Bull dearly and could not wait to see him again.

However, her joy was also her downfall. For it made her forget his instructions, and move one foot over the other. By the time she realized her foolish mistake, it was too late.

For though the Black Bull, on his way back from battle, tried his best to return to the place where he had left her, uncanny powers beyond his control led him astray. The girl waited and waited for him, weeping to exhaustion, but they never found each other.

*****

Thus, wretchedly, the night passed. By morning, the poor girl assumed there was no hope left. So she made her way out of the gloomy valley to a wide-open plain, where the only road led to a single, towering mountain. She walked steadily towards it, but when she reached the mountain, she had to stop. For there was no way round it on either side; and though the road continued up the mountain, from that point on it was formed of slippery glass.

For a long while she gazed up at it, feeling sick at heart. However, she was standing by a forge and now the blacksmith came out, wiping his hands on a cloth.

'Are you in trouble?' he asked her.

'Yes,' she said. 'You see, it's vital I climb this mountain, to find the one I love more than anything in the whole wide world. But that's impossible, as the road is made of glass.'

'Who's your lover and why has he deserted you?' asked the blacksmith.

She did not admit she had fallen in love with a bull, for fear of being mocked. So she said: 'He's vanished under a terrible enchantment, and only I can save him.'

'In that case, I pity you,' said the blacksmith. 'Would you like me to make you a pair of spiked iron shoes, strong enough to climb the glass? It's a difficult task that will take seven long years; but I'm willing to undertake it, if you'll work hard for me every day throughout that time.'

The girl, realizing this was her only hope, readily agreed.

She spent the next seven years working like a slave for the blacksmith without ever once complaining. At the end of that time, the blacksmith put the finished shoes into her hands, and wished her good luck.

*****

The girl – now blossomed into a valiant young woman – easily climbed the glass mountain in her iron shoes. At the top, she saw a castle in the

distance, and a cottage close by. Standing at the door of this cottage was a weary-looking washer-wife and her pretty daughter.

'Good morning,' the young woman greeted them.

'It's not a good morning for us,' said the washer-wife mournfully. 'You see, the gallant young Black Knight from the castle has brought us his best shirt to wash, covered in bright red bloodstains which seem impossible to remove. He badly wants that shirt to be cleaned, and has promised that if any young woman succeeds in doing so, he'll marry her, no matter how humble her origins. Since we're experts at washing, we felt sure my daughter here could win him in this way. Marrying such a wealthy man would bring an end to all our troubles! But though she's been trying for days, she can't make any progress.'

'If I help,' said the young woman, 'would you let me stay with you tonight? For I'm weary from climbing this mountain and have nowhere else to go.'

'There's nothing to be lost by you trying,' said the washer-wife.

She led the young woman behind the cottage to a tub of soapy water, with a scrubbing brush on the table beside it. 'The shirt's in there,' said she.

The young woman rolled up her sleeves, went to the tub and set to work at once. She pulled out the sopping wet shirt, and saw it was indeed covered in bloody stains. She rubbed the brush vigorously across them, squeezed out the water, repeated this several times, then held up the shirt for them to see.

'That's a miracle!' the washer-wife exclaimed. 'You've got it clean! My dear, you come into the cottage and make yourself comfortable, while we ask the castle to send the knight here to collect his shirt. When he sees it, he'll have to marry my daughter!'

Of course, it was really the young woman who should have been rewarded for the cleansing, not the washer-wife's daughter. However, she had more important matters to worry about, so said nothing.

Later in the day, the Black Knight arrived to collect the shirt, which they had now dried in the wind and neatly folded up. The young woman was startled to see that his armour was exactly as black as her lost bull's hair; and his crooning voice was the same as the bull's voice. However, he did not even notice her, having been told it was the washer-wife's daughter who had cleansed his shirt free of blood. When he saw with his own eyes that this was true, he promised to marry her at once and galloped off to organize their wedding.

The young woman was in great distress that night as she bedded down in the washer-wife's cottage. Then she remembered the red apple in her bag. Surreptitiously, she brought it out, cracked it open – and was astonished to find it full of silver jewellery. An idea at once took shape in her mind. She showed the jewellery to the washer-wife's daughter, saying, 'Would you like to wear this to pretty yourself up when you get married? You can have it, if you'll persuade the knight to delay your wedding for a day.'

The daughter readily agreed, and soon fell fast asleep clutching the silver. Then the young woman crept from the cottage, ran to the castle, sneaked inside, found her way to the Black Knight's room, opened the door and went to stand by his bed. He was fast asleep, so she sang loudly to awaken him:

> *Seven long years I toiled for you,*
> *The glass mountain I climbed for you,*
> *The blood-stained shirt I washed for you,*
> *Wake up, my love, and turn to me!*

But the Black Knight did not even stir. For the crafty washer-wife had guessed the young woman would want to claim the knight for herself, and had secretly visited him for this purpose. She had gone to the palace earlier on, disguised as a maid, and taken a drink to the knight which she had laced with sleeping potion. Because of this, though the young woman continued to sing and beg him at the top of her voice, he did not wake up at all. When dawn broke, she was forced to leave him and creep back to the cottage.

There the young woman stayed for another day and night, continuing to help with the washer-wife's work. That night, she cracked open the pear from her bag and found it full of golden jewellery. She showed this to the washer-wife's daughter, saying, 'You can wear this at your wedding, if you'll persuade the knight to delay it for another day.'

Again, the daughter readily agreed; and again, the young woman crept out to the Black Knight's bedside. Again, she sang to him all through the dark hours; and again he failed to awaken due to the washer-wife's sleeping potion. Just as on the previous night, the young woman returned to the cottage in despair.

She now broke open the plum from her bag and found it full of gleaming precious stones. The washer-wife's daughter eagerly accepted these in return for a final delay to her wedding. Nevertheless, the young woman had little hope of ever being able to tell the Black Knight the truth.

*****

Luckily, however, the Black Knight was not the only one who slept in that castle, for the rooms on either side of his were occupied by two young lords. The following morning, these three went out hunting together. As they fitted arrows to their bows, one of them said to the Black Knight, 'Who is the lady that sings by your bedside? Is she your secret lover?'

The knight looked at him in surprise. 'Lady? I assure you that I always sleep alone.'

'Then you must be deaf,' said the other young lord. 'Her sweet voice has disturbed us for two nights now, not to mention her sorrowful moaning.'

This made the knight think back over what had happened on the previous two evenings. He remembered how a maid he had never seen before had brought him a drink before he settled down, and his suspicions were aroused.

So that evening, when the maid – who, of course, was really the washer-wife – brought him her potion, he told her to leave it on his table

so he could drink it slowly. As soon she had gone, he poured it out of the window.

He then got into bed, and this time had no trouble in staying awake. When the young woman crept into his room and began her sad song, he leaped up at once, crying, 'Is it really you? Who I carried on my back past my three brothers' castles? Who waited patiently while I fought the Devil, but who I failed to find again, despite the strength of my love?'

'It is me indeed,' she replied, 'and despite my foolish mistake, I swear my love is as strong as yours.'

He held out his hand. The young woman accepted it and let him take her into his arms.

They spent the rest of the dark hours telling each other everything that had happened since she waited while he battled against the Devil. He explained that victory had freed him from enchantment and enabled him to return to his true form and old home. He said that, despite this, he had never stopped grieving for the loss of her; and she said she had always felt the same about him. As for the bloodstained shirt, it was the kindly old witch from the beginning of this story who gave it to him, saying that no one could ever wash it clean except for his long-lost sweetheart. He had not really believed that the washer-wife's daughter was the one, but had no way until now to discover the truth.

The next morning, the Black Knight cancelled his wedding to the washer-wife's daughter and ordered the pair of them to be seized and punished for their cruel deceit.

He then married the valiant young woman who was the true love of his life. And, so far as anyone knows, they are still living happily together to this very day.

The Daughter
of King Under-Wave

IRELAND AND SCOTLAND

here was a grand house in a valley under a hill where the elite members of the Fianna – the High King's warriors – lived alongside their leader, mighty Fionn mac Cumhaill. One snowy winter's night, these bold men were woken by a boisterous knocking at their door. Before any could rise to open it, the door was flung wide open and a wild-looking old woman came in, staggering like a drunkard. Her face was twisted into an angry grimace, her filthy, ash-grey hair hung in a matted tangle down to her ankles, her tattered dress was covered in slimy mud and she stank of dead mice and rotten fish.

The Fianna all stared at her in disgust as she stumbled up to Fionn's bed, cackling, 'Fionn, let me under your blanket!'

'Go away, old hag!' he retorted. 'Don't soil my bed with your filth!'

The old woman let out a harsh screech that chilled all their bones to the core. Then she made her way to Oisín's bed.

'Oisín,' she croaked, 'let me under your blanket!'

'Get lost, old crone,' he answered quickly, 'Keep your muck away!'

Again she gave a bone-chilling screech, then went to Caoilte's bed. 'Caoilte,' she rasped, 'let me under your blanket!'

'No!' he exclaimed. 'Keep off me!'

For a third time she screeched, then went to Diarmaid's bed.

'Diarmaid,' she croaked, 'will *you* let me under your blanket?'

Diarmaid stared at her, wide-eyed; but he answered pityingly, 'You poor, wretched old woman! Yes, you can come under my blanket, so long as it's not too close.'

The old woman heaved herself onto his bed and lay there shivering on the edge, while Diarmaid huddled away from her on the far side.

After a while she said hoarsely, 'I've travelled over land and sea for seven long years, and every man I met on the way rejected me like your three companions. You're the first to give me shelter, Diarmaid: you're a good man. But I'm still freezing. Will you take me to the fire and stoke it up to warm me?'

Again, Diarmaid did not refuse her. The other Fianna lay watching silently from their beds, holding their noses against her stink. The old woman squatted by Diarmaid's side and held out her scraggy fingers to the flames. After a while she said, 'Diarmaid, shall we go back to your bed now – and this time lie a little closer?'

The other men sniggered. But Diarmaid steadfastly led the way back, got into bed and held up the blanket for the old woman to clamber in properly beside him.

They both lay there on their backs, very still. After a while, Diarmaid glanced surreptitiously across at her – and got the shock of his life. For the repulsive old woman had suddenly transformed – into the most beautiful lady he had ever seen or even dreamed of! Her skin was white and soft as foam on a summer wave, her hair like yellow butter, her cheeks and lips like rose petals.

Diarmaid and the lady lay peacefully side by side for a long while. Then suddenly she nudged him with slim, gentle fingers, whispering, 'Diarmaid! Are you awake?'

'I am,' he answered at once.

'Then tell me,' she said, 'would you like to see the best house ever built since the beginning of time, standing on the hill above this valley?'

'I would,' said he.

'Then go back to sleep and you shall have it.'

After that, awash in her dew-sweet scent, he slumbered deeply until dawn. Then the lady wakened him saying, 'Diarmaid, come and see the house I promised you.'

He followed her outside. Sure enough, there on the hill above them was a brand-new house, with oak walls, thick heather thatch and beautifully carved door pillars.

'No doubt you want to come up and see it?' she said. 'But before you do, I'm going to lay a geis on you. I forbid you to ever mention how hideous I looked the first time you saw me.'

'Of course I won't,' he cried.

'So you claim,' she said. 'But your will is weaker than you think, Diarmaid, and you can't always control your temper. Because of this, I'll give you two chances. If you break this geis twice, I'll forgive you. But if you do so a third time, then everything we have together will be lost.'

'There'll never be cause for that,' he assured her.

So she led him up the hill to their new home, with his faithful greyhound bitch bounding after them accompanied by her three young pups. When they went inside, Diarmaid found splendid furnishings, bustling servants and the table generously laid with beef, cheese, honey, butter and loaves of new-baked bread. There was also a bowl of meaty bones for the dogs.

And there Diarmaid settled down to live with his new lady. At first, he was completely happy.

However, when they rose on the third morning, his lady said, 'Diarmaid, you seem restless today. I can tell you miss your comrades. Why don't you pay them a visit?'

'I'd like to,' he said. 'But will you take good care of my greyhound and her pups till I return?'

'Don't worry about a thing,' said she.

So Diarmaid went off to join the other Fianna in the valley. There was so much to tell them about his lover and their new home, he did not notice that their leader, Fionn himself, was not amongst them.

For when Fionn saw Diarmaid leaving the house on the hill, he seized the opportunity to visit the beautiful lady himself. She gave him a warm welcome, saying, 'Come right in, Fionn, and share some wine with me.'

'Only if you'll give me one of those fine pups I see in the room behind you,' he said.

She nodded, saying, 'Choose whichever one you want and take it back with you.'

So he did.

When Diarmaid returned at dusk, his greyhound bitch greeted him with a mournful yelp. He saw that there were only two pups left in her basket, and fell into a fury. He called the lady to come forward and scolded her: 'You said you'd take care of my pups, but you broke your word. If you remembered how disgusting you looked when I first set eyes on you, you'd not risk losing my love with this lie!'

'Diarmaid,' she threw back at him. 'In saying this, you've broken the *geis* I laid on you. One of the chances I gave you is already lost!'

He apologized and she accepted it; then she apologized for giving away the pup and he accepted that; and it was an excellent night they enjoyed together afterwards.

The next day, Diarmaid visited his comrades again. While he was away Oisín paid the lady a visit, had a drink of wine with her, then asked for one of Diarmaid's pups. Again, she willingly let him take it. When Diarmaid returned, the bitch greeted him with two mournful yelps; for now there was now only one pup left in her basket.

This time he carefully said nothing of his fury to the lady herself. However, as he comforted the faithful bitch, he whispered in her ear, 'My lover broke her word again. If she remembered what a monster she was when I first set eyes on her, she'd not risk losing my love in this way!'

Despite his efforts at discretion, the lady overheard him. 'Diarmaid,' she said, 'control your anger. If you repeat those forbidden words one more time, you will lose me!'

So they forgave each other once more, swearing not to cause any hurt ever again. But as on the previous occasions, the lady provoked him by giving away his last pup to Caoilte while Diarmaid was visiting his comrades.

When he returned that night, he found his faithful bitch in extreme distress, not just yelping three times but also whining, biting her tail and doing all manner of other sorrowful things. So he marched up to the lady and said to her face, 'Shame on you! I accepted you at the beginning as an ugly old hag, yet you return my kindness by giving away my treasured pups!'

'Diarmaid,' she replied, 'you should have held your tongue. Everything is totally lost now. We'll never have the chance to love each other again!'

The next moment, she vanished. And the moment after that, the splendid house vanished too, leaving Diarmaid standing alone on the bare ground, with only his whimpering greyhound bitch for company.

*****

Diarmaid was devastated. Telling the greyhound to wait quietly until he returned, he set off in search of his lady.

His path took him through a long, lonely valley, all the way to the edge of the sea. There he saw a ship moored a little way out. He thrust his spear into the ground, leaned on the handle and used this to leap lightly on board. The ship had neither crew nor passengers, but it carried him to the far shore, where he clambered out, lay down and fell asleep.

The next morning he walked along a broad, empty plain. On his way, he noticed a drop of spilled blood on the ground. Thinking it might be significant, he carefully scooped it into the small bottle he wore at his belt. A little way further along, he found a second drop of blood, then a third. He scooped these up too.

He went on, further and further through this lonely place, until he spotted an old woman standing on the edge of a lake. She was gathering rushes, working in a frenzy, wrenching them quickly from the damp shore and tossing them into a basket as if her life depended on it.

'Good morning!' he called. Can you tell me what country I find myself in?'

She glanced up at him as she worked, saying breathlessly, 'This is King Under-Wave's land.'

He thanked her and asked why she was working so hard.

'Because the king's daughter is in terrible need of these rushes,' the old woman replied. 'She was under an evil enchantment for seven long years, and now she's managed to escape it and return home – but she's seriously ill. Though all the doctors in the land are gathered there, none can do anything to cure her, except to recommend she lies in a soft rush bed.'

As soon as he heard that the daughter of King Under-Wave had recently escaped an enchantment, Diarmaid guessed she was his own beloved lady. 'Will you take me to the king's daughter?' he asked. 'I may be able to help her.'

'If only you could, sir!' said the old woman. 'But there are so many charlatans about that the king won't let anyone near her except her own servants and the doctors. Never mind, wait while I bind the rushes here into a sheaf, then climb inside it. I'll carry you to the palace in that and smuggle you in.'

Diarmaid hesitated, worrying he was too heavy. However, the old woman insisted, and once he was mounted on her back inside the sheaf of rushes, she strode to her master's palace without once having to stop or put him down. The gatekeepers nodded her inside, and the same thing happened at the door of the royal hall. Thus in no time at all, Diarmaid was standing inside the bedchamber of the daughter of King Under-Wave. Fortunately, no one else was in attendance, for the king had just dismissed all the doctors in disgrace.

The old woman deposited the rushes on the floor. Diarmaid stepped out of them and approached the bed. There he immediately recognized his beloved lady, who looked as beautiful as ever, yet pale and wan as a winter moon.

'So you've found me, Diarmaid,' said she.

'I have indeed, my lady,' he said. 'And I apologize with all my heart for breaking the *geis* you laid upon me. I swear it was not my intention to do so, for I had hoped to live with you forever.'

She accepted his apology, saying, 'Because you managed to find me here, three parts of my sickness have already gone and I'm feeling quite a bit better.' She sat up and took his hand. 'But unfortunately, the fourth and final part can never be healed. Because during my long journey back here to my father's country, I could not help grieving for you; and each time I did so, a drop of blood fell from my heart – three drops in all. I will never be cured unless I find them and drink them back into my body,'

At this, Diarmaid cried, 'My lady, I found these very drops on my way here. And – look! – I put them in this little bottle.' He held it out to her. 'Drink them at once!'

'Thank you, Diarmaid,' she replied. 'But unfortunately, the blood in itself is not enough. For to be cured, I need to drink them from a special cup of healing that is impossible to obtain. Many men have already sought it, and all have failed.'

'I will not fail you,' Diarmaid assured her. 'Tell me where this cup can be found, and I'll fetch it.'

'It belongs to the King of the Plain of Wonder,' she said. 'His palace stands not far from the boundary of my father's country, yet is impossible to reach. For our lands are separated by a river which, though narrow, can only be crossed after first sailing a ship up and down it for a whole year and a day, with the wind always blowing from behind.'

Diarmaid set off to find the impassable river at once. It did not take him long; but there was no sign there of the ship his lady had spoken of. Just as he began to despair, he heard a voice calling him, low and creaking as a rusty hinge: 'Diarmaid, grandson of Duibhne – I've been expecting you!'

A squat man with a tangle of dark red beard and hair was standing in the water just upstream. He waded closer, saying, 'Put your foot in the palm of my hand and I'll carry you across.'

This was done. When Diarmaid was standing on dry land again, the little red-headed man said, 'It's the palace of the King of the Plain of Wonder you're heading for, is it not? I'll take you there, and also help you as much as I can when we arrive.'

So Diarmaid and the little red-headed man walked side by side across the wide plain. At last, they reached the high walls of a great fort, with the royal palace inside.

'Now,' said the little red-headed man, 'shout out your request. You've come for the King of the Plain of Wonder's cup, haven't you? Make sure they know it and say that if he won't give it to you willingly, you'll fight for it.'

Diarmaid relished winning a battle as much as any man in the Fianna. So he bellowed, 'Great king! I order you to bring out your fabled cup of healing at once! I won't accept "no" for an answer, so if you don't want to give it to me, send out your army instead!'

For a long while, nothing happened. Then suddenly, the gates of the fort burst open and out marched twice times nine hundred heavily armed warriors. Diarmaid was standing ready with his spear and sword, and eagerly faced them single-handed. In less than three hours, he had defeated them all.

But still the King of the Plain of Wonder refused to yield his cup, instead sending out a second army, this one twice as large as the previous one. After four hours of fighting, Diarmaid had defeated them too.

Then the King of the Plain of Wonder himself came out to stand upon the ramparts, roaring, 'Who is the man who just destroyed both my armies?'

'It is me, Diarmaid, from the Fianna of Ireland,' he shouted back.

'Ach,' said the king, 'Diarmaid is it? Why ever did you not send word ahead that you were on your way? For it has long been prophesied that a champion of the Fianna would come. If I'd known it was you, I wouldn't have wasted all my men trying to repel you. So you want my cup of healing, do you? Don't cause any more damage – just take it!'

He disappeared from the ramparts and soon appeared at the open gate, holding a large golden cup, engraved with swirling patterns and mounted with dark red gemstones. He put it into Diarmaid's hands, and Diarmaid accepted it gladly.

The little red-headed man now led Diarmaid away and they retraced their steps until they saw the river that they had previously crossed together.

'Now,' said the little red-headed man, 'you have a difficult choice, Diarmaid. Firstly, I can carry you straight back to the far side with the cup. If I do that, when you take it to your lady, she will thank you for it and put inside it the three drops of her lost blood that she lost and you then found. But she will not be able to drink them, so will never recover from her illness, no matter how much love you shower on her.

'The alternative is for me to first take you to a well where you can fill the cup with magic water. If she mixes the blood with this water in the cup, then drinks three draughts of it, she will be instantly and permanently cured.'

'Obviously, we must do that!' cried Diarmaid.

'Not so fast,' said the little red-headed man. 'For there is a price to pay for this complete cure. As soon as she drinks the blood mixed with magic water from the cup of healing, you yourself will stop loving her. You will never regain the feelings you once felt for her.

'So, my friend. Would you prefer everlasting love for a lady destined to die within a month? Or to permanently lose your love for her, while she grows healthier and more beautiful by the hour? Only you can decide.'

Diarmaid thought long and hard, imagining first one way and then the other. But in truth, he had no choice at all.

So he went to the magic well with the little red man and filled the King of the Plain of Wonder's cup with its magic water. Then the little red-headed man carried him back across the river, and on the far bank he bid Diarmaid farewell.

Diarmaid travelled on alone to the palace of King Under-Wave. There he was shown to his lady's bedchamber and gave her the cup of healing filled with the magic water.

His lady poured her lost drops of blood into it and drank: once, twice, three times. As soon as she had swallowed the last draught, the colour returned to her face and she leaped, smiling, from her bed. Truly, if she had been lovely, lithe and charming before, now she was nine times more so.

But when Diarmaid gazed at her after that, just as the little red-headed man had warned, his heart felt cold and empty.

The lady thanked him for his help and self-sacrifice with lingering affection in her voice. But Diarmaid just turned his back on her and did not even answer.

King Under-Wave expressed his gratitude to Diarmaid over and over, offering him priceless rewards, including his daughter's hand in marriage. But Diarmaid said that he could not accept any of them, least of all her – for he never wished to set eyes on her again. All he wanted now was a ship to speedily transport him back to Ireland so he could be reunited with the Fianna.

This was arranged for him at once. And when he arrived home, all his comrades greeted him with unbridled joy; but none more so than his faithful greyhound.

Notes to the Stories

It is in the nature of fairy tales and legends that there are no 'correct' versions, since they constantly evolve in the hands of each new narrator.

For the retellings here I have used the oldest sources I could find; these are shown in the notes to each individual story. In bringing them back to life for modern readers, I have sometimes combined several different versions, and where these are confusing, I have subtly adapted them to make more sense. However, I have always taken care to remain true to the original plots, characters and spirit of the old storytellers.

The Sorceress and the Poet

Charlotte Guest: *The Mabinogion*

The earliest surviving manuscript of this legend seems to be the mid-16th-century *Hanes Taliesin* (The Tale of Taliesin) by Elis Gruffydd. Another version was written by John Jones of Gellilyfdy in the early 17th century. Guest, who worked from later manuscripts, included it in her 1877 translations of medieval Welsh stories known as *The Mabinogion*. Subsequent translators of *The Mabinogion* omitted this tale, perhaps because it seems to be of considerably later date than the others.

Some commentators have claimed that Caridwen was an ancient Celtic goddess, though there is nothing to support this in Guest's translated text.

The original account is rather muddled, suggesting that those who wrote it down had attempted to cobble together several different versions, or perhaps even different oral stories. It goes into some detail about

Elffin's dysfunctional relationship with his parents, and is ambiguous about their social status; initially it depicts them as peasants, yet a few pages later says they are related to the provincial king, Maelgwn. It also contains a distracting episode in which Elffin says his wife is more honourable than the queen, with the king sending his son to test her virtue, and Taliesin playing a malicious trick to justify the claim. The latter part comprises long sections of obscure poetry.

My retelling omits these complexities, in order to clarify the central plot and emphasize Taliesin's significance in Welsh tradition. The poems Taliesin recites here are inspired by the cryptic and very verbose originals.

A number of poems that claim to be the work of a man called Taliesin appear in a 14th-century manuscript known as *The Book of Taliesin*. According to the website of the National Library of Wales, he was a real man who lived towards the end of the 6th century. He apparently composed poems in praise of King Urien of Rheged and his son Owain. Rheged was not actually a Welsh kingdom, but based in northwest England and southwest Scotland. Maelgwn is presumed to be a real 6th-century king, whose death was recorded several hundred years later in *Annales Cambriae* ('Chronicles of Wales').

Magic cauldrons are a feature of other old Welsh stories in *The Mabinogion*. In 'Branwen', an Irish king cooks his dead warriors in a cauldron overnight; the next morning they are reborn with full vigour, though lacking the ability to speak. In 'Culhwch and Olwen', one of the 'impossible' tasks a hero is set in order to win his desired bride is stealing a supernatural cauldron belonging to the King of Ireland. Several other elements are not unique to this story. For example, Gwion Bach's accidental consumption of a forbidden supernatural substance closely echoes Fionn mac Cumhaill's inadvertent tasting of the Salmon of Knowledge (see p.192); whilst the motif of a child cast out on the water, then rescued to its advantage, is common in European folktales.

In pre-literate times, bards were professional male oral historians, genealogists and storytellers, often employed by a high-status patron. The use of verse has parallels in other world cultures and perhaps helped them to commit long passages accurately to memory. The tradition is kept alive today in the annual Welsh-language 'National Eisteddfod of Wales', which claims to be the largest festival of competitive music and poetry in Europe.

The Swan Woman

Jeffrey Gantz: *Early Irish Myths and Sagas*

The earliest known mention of this story, usually known as 'The Dream of Aonghus' (also spelt Óengus) is in the 12th-century *Book of Leinster*, though only as part of a list of preliminary tales to another major myth. The oldest complete recount is in a 15th- or early 16th-century manuscript, currently housed in the British Library in London.

In Irish mythology, Aonghus was one of the Tuatha Dé Danaan, a race of deities who supposedly invaded Ireland in antiquity. Their name means 'people of the goddess Danu'. They were skilled magicians whose power was enhanced by several supernatural objects, including the Stone of Fál, which cried out to verify a legitimate king; the Spear of Lugh, which guaranteed victory; and the Sword of Nuadu, from which no one could escape. Immortal, ageless and beautiful, they lived in the mythical Otherworld, with chiefs or kings, and hierarchies parallel to the mortal world above. Each king of the Tuatha Dé Danaan had his own domain under a hill or mound known as a *sídh*. These are sometimes identified by scholars as Neolithic or Bronze Age graves. According to modern Irish folklore, these are faery mounds.

Aonghus was the god of love, and other myths tell of him helping illustrious couples fulfil illicit liaisons, most notably in the tales of 'Diarmaid and Gráinne' (see p.203), and 'Midhir and Etain'.

Aonghus's father was a powerful, wise yet uncouth king of the Tuatha Dé Danaan, usually called The Dagdae (Daghda). His name means 'the good god' because amongst the miracles he regularly performed was overseeing the harvest. He owned two supernatural objects of his own: a cauldron with inexhaustible contents that could satisfy everyone; and a marvellous, double-ended club, one end of which killed the living, while the other end revived the dead. As mentioned in the story, his courtship of Aonghus's mother, Bóand, was problematic. Though attracted to The Dagdae, she was already married to a fearsome man called Elcmar. The Dagdae sent Elcmar away on a long journey, enchanting him so that he was unaware of the passing of time. Though Elcmar vowed to return before nightfall, in fact his perception of a single day was really nine months. During his absence, The Dagdae made love to Bóand who thus conceived Aonghus. By the time her husband returned, she was fully recovered from the birth, so that he had no idea of her infidelity. The Dagdae had Aonghus raised in secret by another man to avoid any shame between Bóand and her husband.

Cáer Ibormeith and her father, Ethan Anbúail, were said to live in the province of Connacht in western Ireland. In the original text, when Ethan is approached by Aonghus, he says he 'cannot' give him his daughter, claiming that this is because 'her power is greater than mine'. This indicates that her shapeshifting into a swan every other year is not of his making, though most commentators seem to assume that it is a spell cast by her father to stop her marrying.

The timpán Cáer played to the sleeping Aonghus at the beginning of the story was a small musical instrument with between three and eight strings, played with a bow or plectrum. Timpáns are mentioned in a number of ancient texts, which indicate that skilled players were held in high esteem.

Cáer's transformation into a swan takes place at Samhain (Samuin), 1st November. As the ancient Irish new year and the first official day of winter, Samhain brought change, rebirth, the re-establishment of order, and opened the boundary between the real world and the mystical Otherworld.

Bodb, who leads Aonghus to the lake where Cáer and her maidens are standing, is described in the original text as another king of the *sídh*, with wide-ranging knowledge of the area.

The transformation of people into swans is a recurring motif in Irish myths. One tells of Derbforgaill, who falls in love with the legendary hero

Cú Chulainn (see p.192). She and a maidservant transform to swans joined by a gold chain in order to pursue him. He shoots Derbforgaill with a stone from his sling, and when she falls, injured, to the ground, she transforms back to human form. In an attempt to heal the wound he inflicted, he sucks out the stone. However, he cannot avoid tasting her blood in the process, breaking a sacred taboo, and is thus prohibited from sexual relations with her. See also a summary of 'The Children of Lir' on p.195, in which a *sídh* king's jealous third wife turns her three stepsons and single stepdaughter into swans.

Mally Whuppy and the Giant

Katharine Briggs: *A Dictionary of British Folk-Tales in the English Language*
Norah and William Montgomerie: *The Well at the World's End*

Briggs collected this story from Aberdeenshire, whilst the Montgomeries sourced exactly the same one in the Scottish Lowlands.

Tales of giants were popular in Scottish oral tradition. Some from the Highlands feature the interesting detail of some giants' magical ability to remove their souls and hide them. This greatly enhances their power; for the giant cannot be killed until the soul has first been destroyed.

Another colourful story tells of a queen who gives birth to a son while the king is away. Not wishing to name him in her husband's absence, she refers to him only as Nicht Nought Nothing. A short time later, the king, on the way home, comes to a river. He sees no means to get over it until a giant comes along and offers to carry him across. 'What do you want in return for your kindness?' asks the king. 'I want nicht nought nothing,' says the giant. Not realizing that is the nickname of his newborn son, the king readily agrees to this apparently generous offer. When he reaches the queen and discovers the truth, they are both in despair. The giant comes to claim his promised reward, only to be fobbed off with first the cook's son, and then the gardener's son. However, he realizes he is being deceived and seizes Nicht Nought Nothing for himself. As the boy grows up, he and the giant's daughter fall in love. She helps him complete a series of impossible tasks that culminate in the giant destroying himself, enabling the youth and his unlikely lover to escape and find happiness together.

Some tales feature the archetypal young hero, Jack. In one, a destructive two-headed giant challenges Jack to a contest to see which of them can eat the most, with the greedy giant exploding when the boy tricks him into slitting open his own stomach to get rid of the excess food. In another, the giant has no less than seven heads. Jack succeeds in cutting them off, one by one; and when the last one falls, the giant transforms into Jack's long-lost brother.

The heroic deeds Mally Whuppy accomplishes, and the rewards she wins for them, are at odds with the usual gender stereotypes found in British and European folktales. This role reversal is noticeable in a number of other Scottish stories, for example 'The Black Bull of Norroway' (p.160) and 'Kate Crackernuts' (p.60).

The Devil, the Witch and the Faeries

P.H. Emerson: *Welsh Fairy-Tales and Other Stories*

In the introduction to his book, Emerson says he collected the stories in it 'whilst living in Anglesey during the winter 1891–2', explaining that he transcribed them at the time they were recited aloud to him. Anglesey is a large island just off the northwest coast of Wales, today joined to the mainland by two bridges. He says he heard this story from a Welsh pedlar woman and 'its genuineness may be relied upon … The narrator says you seldom hear a fairy story in Anglesey unless there is a witch in it.' Although most British and Irish stories depict faeries as capricious and dangerous, Emerson asserts, 'I have heard of no evil faeries in Wales; all the mischief seems to be the work of witches.'

Nevertheless, the faeries he describes are very different from those of other Welsh tales, some of which name them as belonging to specific tribes, each with its own characteristics. The Bwca and Bwbachod are domestic faeries, similar to Scottish and English Brownies. They are shaggy, diminutive men who helpfully come out at night to do chores within the household or farm; but they are also vengeful and easily offended. Both tribes are said to dislike teetotallers – perhaps revealing more about the storytellers than the actual faeries! Coblynau are small males who haunt mines, and it is considered lucky to see one. Ellylldan are will o' the wisps who lure travellers into bogs. Ellyllon are tiny, translucent elves that live on fungi, ruled by a queen called Mab. Gwyllion are evil female mountain spirits who lead travellers astray at night. The Tylwyth Teg are fair-haired creatures who covet human children of the same colouring; their womenfolk sometimes agree to temporarily marry mortal men. They give gifts to people they approve of, but unless these gifts are kept totally secret, they vanish.

For a Scottish tale of faeries, see 'The Bogle of the Murky Well' (p.126).

Folk tales in which the Devil appears as a useless and often naive trickster are common throughout Britain. Emerson records another one in which a drunkard called Billy sells himself to the Devil in return for seven years' worth of money to buy unlimited alcohol. During that period, a good deed to a stranger wins Billy three wishes in return, and it is these eccentric wishes that enable him to outwit the Devil. When Billy dies, he is refused admission to Hell as well as to Heaven; so he transforms into a ball of fire. Amongst the Welsh stories collected by W. Jenkyn Thomas in 1908 is one in which an old woman is distressed when her cow wades out of reach across a river. She is approached by a man who offers to build a bridge on the spot for her, asking payment of the first living creature to cross it. With a bargain like that, the woman quickly realizes her helper is the Devil. She cunningly throws a crust of bread onto the newly finished bridge, then releases her dog to fetch it. The dog should thus be the Devil's prize, but he rejects it and vanishes.

Amongst Scottish Devil tales is one that features a minister's maidservant courted by an apparently wonderful man – but when she brings him to the house, the minister spots his cloven hooves. At the wedding service, he lights a candle at both ends, says he will marry them when these flames meet in the middle, then swallows the flames before this can happen – thus saving his maid. Another describes how a man frees himself from a foolish bargain struck with the Devil by standing in a circle in the woods at midnight reading the Bible aloud, boldly ignoring distracting visions until the morning. He not only escapes, but finds a bag of gold in the circle.

Witch stories are usually more malicious and misogynous than the one told here. Thomas reports a Welsh one in which travellers staying at a particular inn are regularly robbed despite keeping the doors tightly locked. The culprits turn out to be the landladies, who transform into witches at night. From Scotland comes the tale of two women who offer to make their impoverished friend rich. They tell her to leave a broom in bed beside her husband that night, and sneak out to join them at a witch's coven. But she confides in her husband, who goes out in her place. At the coven, he shouts out the name of God; this destroys everything, and the witches are drowned. Another one features a blacksmith's wife who every night transforms her husband into a horse, which she rides hard all through the hours of darkness on wicked errands, leaving the poor man ill with exhaustion. His elder brother volunteers to take his place, manages to expose her, and has her burned as a witch.

Devil, faery and witch stories are also common in England; see my companion volumes, *English Fairy Tales and Legends* and *Faeries, Elves & Goblins: The Old Stories*.

Fionn mac Cumhaill and the Magic Drinking Horn
P.W. Joyce: *Old Celtic Romances*

This belongs to a set of three ancient tales that were originally written in Gaelic verse. Joyce calls the story 'The Chase of Slieve Fuad', the name once used for the highest of the Fews Mountains in Armagh.

Stories of the legendary leader Fionn mac Cumhaill (Finn macCool) date back to at least the 8th century, reached their height during the 12th century, and have remained popular in both literary texts and folklore ever since. Fionn is portrayed as having superhuman powers in combat, and is strongly linked with the supernatural. For example, one story tells how he obtained wisdom and prescience by accidentally eating the Salmon of Knowledge, which an old seer had been trying to obtain for himself – a very similar motif to the one used in 'The Sorceress and the Poet' from Wales (see p.8). Another describes Fionn using magic to overcome an evil spirit who had been setting fire to a royal palace each year.

Fionn's band of warriors, the Fianna, formed a voluntary army who served the High King of Ireland. In order to be accepted into their ranks, a potential recruit had to survive ordeals such as waist-deep burial while having spears thrown at him; leaping over a stick of equal height to himself then stooping under another that was only knee-high; and removing a thorn from his foot whilst running. He must also learn twelve entire books of poetry off by heart, and publicly denounce all thoughts of revenge. The rewards of membership were high status, good pay and various privileges. Alongside his warriors, Fionn also employed druids, physicians, poets, musicians, cup-bearers, doorkeepers, horn players, stewards, huntsmen, serving men and a team of outstanding seamstresses. Some members of the Fianna had stories of their own; see, for example, 'The Daughter of King Under-Wave' (p.172).

Another celebrated Irish hero was Cú Chulainn, who appears in legends going back as far as the 7th century. Sometimes said to have a divine father, he was associated with the Otherworld, and blessed with supernatural strength. Like Fionn he was the victor of every battle, aided by his magic weapons, and sometimes fighting single-handed against large numbers of enemies.

Kate Crackernuts

Katharine Briggs: *A Dictionary of British Folk-Tales in the English Language*
Gordon Jarvie: *Scottish Folk and Fairy Tales*

This story has obvious parallels to the well-known 'Twelve Dancing Princesses', a German fairy tale collected by the Brothers Grimm. However, as in a number of other Scottish folk tales, the usual gender stereotypes are reversed, so that the victim is a man, and the hero who rescues him is a young woman.

It is common in folk tales to keep the characters anonymous, simply calling them 'a princess', 'a king' and so on. However, here the heroine's name is intrinsic to the story. Jarvie obtained it from Elizabeth Grierson of the Scottish Borders, who names the king's daughter rather cloyingly as 'Princess Velvet Cheek' and the heroine as 'Katherine'. Briggs gives an Orkney version which names *both* girls as Kate; whilst 19th-century folklorist Andrew Lang changed one of their names to 'Anne' when he retold it, presumably to avoid confusion. In my retelling I use the related forms Kate and Katherine to symbolize the girls' spiritual closeness as stepsisters.

A related Scottish tale tells of a girl who sets out to discover why her older sister has vanished. On her journey, she helps two beggars, who then direct her to a wizard's castle. They also give helpful advice on how to withstand the evil one's spells, thus enabling her to rescue her sister. At the end, each marries one of the beggars – who themselves turn out to be bewitched gentlemen.

The Red Dragon

Nennius: *History of the Britons*
Geoffrey of Monmouth: *Histories of the Kings of Britain*

Vortigen may have been a real king, believed by some scholars to have ruled during the mid-5th century. However, accounts of his life and reign were passed down solely by oral tradition for hundreds of years, until Nennius transcribed them in the 9th century (with the oldest surviving manuscripts dating from the 11th century). The same story was told in greater detail in the 12th century by Geoffrey of Monmouth. Both describe Vortigen making a doomed treaty with the Anglo-Saxon invaders who conquered much of England during the 5th to 7th centuries.

Merlin's identity in the legend is somewhat ambiguous. In fact, Nennius does not reveal his name until the end of the episode, when the boy says he is called 'Ambrosius; my father was a Roman consul'. However, Geoffrey, writing some 300 years later, calls him Merlin through most of his account, though mentions that he 'is also called Ambrosius'. It appears that during the intervening centuries, unknown storytellers changed Nennius' original character into one with an unambiguously Welsh background, and gave him a new name. This is an interesting example of how folk narratives develop over numerous retellings, so that there is never any single authentic version.

Geoffrey's long account of Merlin's obscure prophesies inspired later storytellers to make him a full-blown wizard. He was a popular character in medieval stories, which immortalized his role in bringing the legendary King Arthur to the throne. Merlin's use of magic for these purposes is vividly depicted in Thomas Malory's 15th-century masterpiece, *Le Morte d'Arthur*. According to Geoffrey, Arthur's principal court was in 'The City of Legions' on the River Usk in Glamorgan, which has been identified as Caerleon in South Wales.

For a full account of Merlin's legendary exploits, see my companion book, *Arthurian Legends*. This also features the oldest surviving complete Arthurian story, which originated in Wales: 'How Culhwch Won Olwen.'

Mount Eryri, where Vortigen attempts to build his fortress, is better known as Snowden (Welsh *Yr Wyddfa*). Part of a range of jagged peaks, at 1,085 metres it is the highest mountain in both Wales and England.

The shame of Merlin's mother in bearing a child out of wedlock – historically known as a 'bastard' – and the resultant persecution of Merlin by his peers, must be understood in the context of the medieval Church. This restricted the legal rights of illegitimate children and severely tarnished the reputations of both mother and child.

A red dragon has been used as a military and royal emblem in Wales since the 7th century, with many Welsh historical military leaders being personified as 'dragons'. There is a related story about it battling against an enemy white dragon, 'Lludd and Llefelys', from the collection of Welsh narratives known as *The Mabinogion* (see p.184). Its image has formed the national flag of Wales since 1959.

The Twelve Wild Geese

Patrick Kennedy: *The Fireside Stories of Ireland*

This entertaining tale has parallels with a well-known, much more tragic Irish story, 'The Children of Lir'. Here, the second wife of Lir – who is one of the Tuatha Dé Danaan (see p.186) – becomes jealous of her four stepchildren and transforms them into swans for 900 years. When they finally return to human shape, they are old and withered, and die shortly afterwards. Despite claims of this being an ancient Irish myth, the oldest written version only goes back to around the 15th century, and some scholars believe it was absorbed into the Irish canon from older English or French medieval folktales.

Kennedy, writing in the late 19th century, says he obtained 'The Twelve Wild Geese', alongside the other stories in his book, 'from bona fide oral sources'. Nevertheless, he makes no claim to them being exclusively Irish, pointing out their strong similarities to folk tales from other parts of Europe and even Asia.

Two very similar ones were collected in Germany by the famous Brothers Grimm; both feature a bold king's daughter rescuing her brothers from their transformation into ravens. A Polish tale has a princess travelling to the land of Death to free her twelve brothers from the spell which turned them into eagles. The queen's longing for a child with snow-white skin, blood-red cheeks and raven-black hair is exactly the same motif that appears in one of the most popular European fairy tales, 'Snow White'. False and malicious accusations against a bereaved young mother not only also appear in the Welsh myth of Rhiannon from

'The First Branch' of *The Mabinogion*, but also recall an episode from distant Persia (modern Iran) in the *Arabian Nights* story called 'Princess Farizade, The Talking Bird, the Singing Tree and the Golden Water'.

The cotton-grass which the princess must spin and weave is *Eriophorum angustifolium*, also known as bog cotton, which grows widely in Ireland on damp, peaty ground. Its insignificant spring flowers later develop into large fluffy white seed-heads, turning wide stretches of moorland white. In historical times, cotton-grass was used to stuff pillows and mattresses.

The Secret World of the Seals

Elizabeth W. Grierson: *The Scottish Fairy Book*
William G. Stewart: *The popular Superstitions and Festive Amusements of the Highlanders of Scotland*

'Roane' is the Scottish Gaelic name for the species of marine shapeshifters that normally take the form of seals, but cast off their skins to appear as humans when they need to. They have been described as 'the gentlest of all faery people', known for not harbouring resentment against humans who offend them.

They are closely related to the 'selkies', whose stories are mainly told in the northern Scottish islands of Orkney and Shetland, where narrative traditions tend to be more Nordic than Celtic. Like roane, selkies can change between human and animal form, but the latter is dependent on them wearing a removable sealskin. A common story is of a selkie women captured by a mortal man who steals her sealskin and persuades her to marry him. She appears to settle down with her human husband, but is secretly unhappy. Eventually she finds where her husband has hidden the stolen skin, puts it on and returns to her true shape, enabling her to go back to her watery home. The roles are reversed with male selkies, who are said to habitually lust after mortal women whom they court, then quickly abandon. Children born with webbed hands and feet are said to be the issue of such unions. In contrast to the roane, stories tell of selkies practising vengeance on seal hunters, raising storms to sink their boats.

Two species of seal live off the coast of Scotland: common (or harbour) seals and grey seals. The larger grey seals spend most of their time feeding at sea, returning to rest on beaches and rocks. Weighing up to 300kg and measuring up to 2 metres in length, their main food is sand eels, supplemented by other species including the spiny fish known as sea-scorpion. Common, or harbour, seals can grow up to 1.5 metres in length, and weigh up to 100kg. They feed on fish, squids, whelks, crabs and mussels. They can often be seen hauled out on sandbanks and beaches in sheltered shores and estuaries. Both species can live for up to thirty years.

The Most Ancient Creature in the World

P.H. Emerson: *Welsh Fairy-Tales and Other Stories*
W. Jenkyn Thomas: *The Welsh Fairy Book*

This short folk tale has roots in the much older and longer 'Culhwch and Olwen', a legend recorded in *The Mabinogion* (see p.184). Here, neither eagle nor owl are central characters; alongside the stag and the blackbird, as some of the oldest and wisest wild creatures in the world, they merely fulfil the role of enabling the hero of the tale to complete a seemingly impossible quest, with the salmon making the most important contribution. This legend is retold in full in my companion book, *Arthurian Legends*. It is interesting to see how subsequent storytellers spun that thread into a more profound tale without any human protagonists.

An eagle is at the centre of another Welsh folktale that is also devoid of human characters. Here, all the birds are choosing a new ruler, and agree that the office will be awarded to the one who can fly the highest. No one is surprised when the muscular Eagle appears to be the winner; but just as he is about to claim the prize, a little voice cries out, 'I've beaten you!' It turns out to be tiny Wren, who had played the trick of riding on Eagle's back and flying a little higher at the last minute. The infuriated Eagle hurls his rival to the ground. The other birds weep with sympathy, and decide to use their tears to heal Wren with a herbal brew. However, clumsy Owl knocks over the pot with his wing. As a result, Wren still has a clipped tail. And – in real life – other birds still show their annoyance by mobbing owls that appear in daylight.

King Cormac and the Golden Apples

Vernam Hull: *Echtra Cormaic Maic Airt, The Adventure of Cormac Mac Airt*
Whitley Stokes: 'Cormac's Adventure in the Land of Promise'
Augusta Gregory: *Complete Irish Mythology*
Joseph Jacobs: *Celtic Fairy Tales, Volume II*

The oldest surviving sources of this story both date from the late 14th century: *The Book of Ballymote* and the *Yellow Book of Lecan,* which are very similar in content. Linguistic analysis of these texts suggests that the original narrative may be at least two hundred years older. Some later versions include extra details reminiscent of well-known fairy tales, for example a tablecloth which magically produces food. In the sources, the story structure is somewhat confused and illogical, so my retelling retains all their important elements but rearranges them a little to clarify sense and meaning.

Based on ancient texts, scholars believe King Cormac Mac Airt – also known as 'grandson of Conn of the Hundred Battles' – reigned in the 3rd century. He supposedly held office for forty years, finally choking to death on a salmon bone. It was claimed that he owned a sword that shone in the dark like a candle, and sharp enough to cut a single hair floating in the water. According to old records, he established the splendour of Tara, legendary seat of Ireland's High Kings, bringing fortune and extraordinary prosperity to the country. The hill of Tara (Irish *Teamhair* or *Temuir*) in County Meath is an ancient ceremonial and burial site containing numerous prehistoric earthworks. Today it is a protected national monument under the care of the Irish government. The hero Fionn mac Cumhaill (see 'The Magic Drinking Horn' p.48) was said to have lived at the same time as Cormac and to have had dealings with him.

Manannán mac Lir ('son of the sea') is described in some later stories as one of the Tuatha Dé Danaan. His domain is usually said to be the ocean, with the waves as his horses. Some poetic texts use the expression 'the locks of Manannán's wife' to portray the waves. See also 'The Daughter of King Under-Wave (p.172).

Visits by legendary heroes to supernatural 'Otherworlds' is a common theme in Irish myths. Alongside Manannán's Land of Promise, these include the Island of Joy and the Land of Women. Perhaps the best known is Tir na Nog, the Land of Eternal Youth; another is the Plain of Delight. A common feature of such stories is that the hero believes he has lived there for only a year; but on returning to the real world discovers to his dismay that several centuries have passed. Such tricks of time are also common in stories featuring mortals abducted by faeries.

The Bogle of the Murky Well

Katharine Briggs: *A Dictionary of British Folk-Tales in the English Language*
Norah and William Montgomerie: *The Well at the World's End*

Perhaps the earliest transcription of this oral tale comes from the Montgomeries, who described how they sourced the narratives in their 1956 collection as follows:

We have sat with the travellers … listening till long after midnight to their Lowland tales, driving home in the dark through an Angus mist so thick the trees by the roadside were invisible. We have listened to, and recorded, Jeannie Robertson in Aberdeen singing the traditional ballads and songs which had come to her from her mother, and not from books. The stories in this book, all of them, came originally out of that world of storytellers and singers. For many years they were passed on from one storyteller to another.

The repeated verses in the tale presumably reflect the 'sung' elements in the old narrators' performances.

According to Briggs, the miller was based at a place called Cuthilldorie. This is possibly the modern Cuthill located near Dornoch on the coast of northeast Scotland. The Montgomeries add a detail about the bogle, saying he was two-and-a-half feet (76cm) high.

The bizarre, malicious nature of the faeries here is typical of British and Irish stories, and faery queens who abduct both adult and infant mortals are common in Scottish tales. Contrast the faeries here with the benevolent ones of the Welsh tale, 'The Devil, the Witch and the Faeries' (p.38); and see my companion book, *Faeries, Elves & Goblins*.

The Sleeping King

Kevin Crossley-Holland: *Folk-Tales of the British Isles* (reproducing a story collected in 1850)
William Elliot Griffis: *Welsh Fairy Tales*
Gwyn Jones: *Welsh Legends and Folk-Tales*
W. Jenkyn Thomas: *The Welsh Fairy Book*

This is a popular legend in Wales. Another version says that the sleeping king is not Arthur, but Owain Lawgoch – a descendant of the powerful ancient Welsh prince Llywelyn the Great. Owain is supposed to be awaiting his appointed time to reclaim the entire British realm.

The location of the sleeping king's cave is sometimes said to be a place called Craig-y-Dinas (Fortress Rock), a spectacular geological formation in the modern Brecon Beacons (Bannau Brycheiniog) National Park in south Wales. Other narrators claim it is variously in Glamorgan, Carmarthenshire or Denbighshire.

Very similar stories about a sleeping king are told far beyond Wales. Versions from Northumberland and Yorkshire agree he is Arthur; but in Irish and Scottish versions the king and his heroes are often Fionn mac Cumhaill and the Fianna (see pp.48 and 172). Similar legends come from all over Europe, each one featuring the country's own local hero.

For more about King Arthur and the Knights of the Round Table, see my companion book, *Arthurian Legends*.

The Merrows' Song

Gordon Jarvie: *Irish Folk and Fairy Tales*

Jarvie names the original narrator of this story as Mary Patton. There is a manuscript in her name in the National Folklore Collection of Ireland, giving her location as County Donegal.

Mary's original narrative is quite long, and goes into some detail about Eonín's family. She located her story near the village of Cill Rónáin (Kilronan) on Inishmore, the largest of the Aran Islands off the west coast of Ireland. She calls the sea people 'mermaids'. However, the correct Irish name for them is 'merrows' – as described by W.B. Yeats in his book *Fairy and Folk Tales of the Irish Peasantry*:

The Merrow, of if you write it in the Irish, Moruadh or Murúghach, from muir, sea, and oigh, a maid, is not uncommon, they say, on the wilder coasts. The fishermen do not like to see them, for it always means coming gales ... Their women are beautiful, for all their fish tails and the little duck-like scale between their fingers. Sometimes they prefer ... good-looking fishermen to their sea lovers.

He says there are also male merrows which have 'green teeth, green hair, pig's eyes, and red noses'.

Conger eels are snake-like, scaleless fish which can grow up to two metres long. Their wide mouths have strong teeth and they have been known to attack humans. They usually live in holes in the rocks, coming out at night to hunt fish and shellfish. Grey seals are common in Irish waters (see p.197). Skerdmore is a tiny, rocky sea island, some way north of the Aran Islands.

A Scottish mermaid story tells of a fisherman who meets and courts a mermaid, and in return for his affection, she brings him treasures. However, when he starts handing this out to the local girls, she becomes jealous, lures him away and makes him her prisoner. In a Welsh tale, a man captures a mermaid and initially refuses to let her go. However, he grants her freedom in return for her warning him of future dangers, and later she saves him from a storm.

The Black Bull of Norroway

Robert Chambers: *Popular Rhymes of Scotland*
Norah and William Montgomerie: *The Well at the World's End*

The tale of a young woman's search for her lost lover, bewitched to shapeshift between human and animal form, occurs in many parts of Europe including Ireland, and has developed into variants in North America and Jamaica. It is related to the Norwegian tale, 'East of the Sun and West of the Moon', in which the bewitched lover is a bear, and which also includes the motif of the young woman proving herself by cleansing a magically stained shirt; perhaps that is why this tale is set in Norway.

The structure of the story, with its repetition and illogical twists and turns, clearly signals its origin as an oral narrative designed to hold listeners' attention and remind them of what has gone before. It is full of classic fairy-tale ingredients such as three siblings setting out on an adventure with only the youngest reaching fulfilment; 'magic helpers' (the kindly witch and the blacksmith); a set of mysterious supernatural objects to be kept until needed; a broken taboo; long journeys; the completion of a seemingly impossible task; and a magic potion. Strong, determined female heroes appear in a number of Scottish folk tales; see also 'Mally Whuppy and the Giant' (p.28) and 'Kate Crackernuts' (p.60).

The Daughter of King Under-Wave

Augusta Gregory: *Lady Gregory's Complete Irish Mythology*

Tales about the hero Fionn mac Cumhaill and his warrior band the Fianna (see p.48) are an inextricable part of Irish tradition; but they were also popular in Scotland. Thus in the notes to her collection, Gregory says she found this story in an earlier book called *Popular Tales of the West Highlands*, by J. F. Campbell, indicating that this was not the only supposedly Irish story that she actually sourced from the Scottish Gaelic. Campbell himself gives his source as a tailor from the Hebridean island of Barra called Roderick MacLean, who in turn had heard it recited orally by elderly men on the neighbouring island of South Uist.

The story motif of the supernatural transformation of an ugly hag into a beautiful woman echoes the English Arthurian legend 'Sir Gawain and the Loathly Lady' and Chaucer's 'The Wife of Bath's Tale'. It is impossible to know which is the original, for folk tales constantly move across borders.

Diarmaid is one of the most prominent members of the Fianna, playing the leading male role in a number of Irish and Scottish romances. He is often described as being irresistibly attractive to women, due to a 'love-spot' on his forehead or neck.

The most famous of these legends tells of his affair with the beautiful Gráinne, who falls in love with Diarmaid despite being already betrothed to Fionn mac Cumhaill himself. When he tries to refuse her, she binds him with a *geis* which forces him to take her away from the court of Tara. Fionn then pursues them all over Ireland, but they manage to keep ahead of him thanks to assistance from the god Aonghus (see 'The Swan Woman', p.20), who is Diarmaid's foster-father. After seven years of unsuccessful pursuit, Fionn pardons Diarmaid, but still deeply resents him, and eventually helps fulfil a prophesy that his opponent will be killed by a supernatural boar.

A *geis*, plural *geissi* (*geas*, plural *geasa*), is a prohibition, an obligation or a bond of honour, similar to a vow or a curse, but with supernatural implications. To break one was to court the inevitability of disaster. It is often used as a narrative device in Irish hero tales. This part of the plot has similarities to a Welsh folk tale, about a man who marries a lake faery, inadvertently breaks his promise not to strike her three times with iron – and thus loses her.

Sources and Further Reading

Briggs, Katharine M.: *A Dictionary of British Folk-Tales in the English Language* (London: Routledge & Kegan Paul, 1970)

Briggs, Katharine: *A Dictionary of Fairies* (London: Allen Lane, 1976)

Campbell, J.F. (translator): *Popular Tales of the West Highlands, orally collected*, Volume III (Paisley and London: Alexander Gardner, 1890)

Chambers, Robert: *Popular Rhymes of Scotland* (Edinburgh and London: W. & R. Chambers Ltd, 1870)

Crossley-Holland, Kevin (editor): *Folk-Tales of the British Isles* (London: Faber and Faber, 1986)

Davies, Sioned (translator): *The Mabinogion* (Oxford University Press, 2007)

Douglas, Sir George: *Scottish Fairy and Folk Tales* (New York: A.L. Burt Company, 1900)

Emerson, P.H.: *Welsh Fairy-Tales and Other Stories* (London: D. Nutt, 1894)

Gantz, Jeffrey (translator): *Early Irish Myths and Sagas* (London: Penguin Books, 1981)

Geoffrey of Monmouth: *Histories of the Kings of Britain,* originally published in the 12th century as 'De gestis Britonum', translated by Sebastian Evans (London: J.M. Dent & Co., 1904. Reprinted by Forgotten Books, 2008.)

Green, Miranda J.: *Dictionary of Celtic Myth and Legend* (London: Thames & Hudson, 1992)

Green, Miranda Jane: *Celtic Myths* (London: British Museum Press, 1993)

Green: Miranda: *Celtic Goddesses: Warriors, Virgins and Mothers* (London: British Museum Press, 1995)

Gregory, Lady Augusta: *Lady Gregory's Complete Irish Mythology* – originally published in London by John Murray in two volumes: 'Cuchulain of Muirthemne', 1902; and 'Gods and Fighting Men', 1904 (New York: Smithmark Publishers, 1996)

Grierson, Elizabeth W.: *The Scottish Fairy Book* (Philadelphia and New York: J.B. Lippincott Company, 1910)

Griffis, William Elliot: *Welsh Fairy Tales* (New York: Thomas Y. Crowell Company, 1921)

Guest, Lady Charlotte (translator): *The Mabinogion,* from the Welsh of the 'Llyfr coch o Hergest' ('The Red Book of Hergest') in the Library of Jesus College, Oxford (London: Bernard Quaritch, 1877)

Hull, Vernam: *Echtra Cormaic Maic Airt — The Adventure of Cormac Mac Airt* (PMLA, Vol. 64, No. 4, Cambridge University Press, 1949)

Jackson, K.H.: *A Celtic Miscellany, Translations from the Celtic Literatures* (London: Penguin Books, 1971)

Jacobs, Joseph: *Celtic Fairy Tales* – originally published in London by David Nutt in two volumes: 'Celtic Fairy Tales', 1892; and 'More Celtic Fairy Tales', 1894 (London: Bracken Books, 1990)

Jarvie, Gordon (editor): *Irish Folk and Fairy Tales* (London: Puffin Books, 1992)

Jarvie, Gordon (editor): *Scottish Folk and Fairy Tales* (London: Puffin Books, 1992)

Jones, Gwyn: *Welsh Legends and Folk Tales* (Oxford University Press, 1955)

Joyce, P.W.: *Old Celtic Romances, translated from the Gaelic* (London: C. Kegan Paul & Co., 1879)

Kennedy, Patrick: *The Fireside Stories of Ireland* (Dublin: M'Glashan and Gill, and Patrick Kennedy, 1870)

Leodhas, Sorche Nic: *Thistle and Thyme, Tales and Legends from Scotland* (London: The Bodley Head, 1965)

Macbain, Alexander (editor): *The Celtic Magazine,* Volume 12, (Inverness, 1887)

Montgomerie, Norah & William: *The Well at the World's End, Folk Tales of Scotland* (London: The Hogarth Press, 1956)

Nennius: *History of the Britons (Historia Brittonum)*, originally written in the 9th century, surviving manuscripts dating from the 11th century, translated by J.A. Giles (Cambridge, Ontario: In parentheses Publications, 2000)

Ó hÓgáin, Dáithí: *Myth, Legend & Romance: An Encyclopædia of Irish Folk Tradition* (London: Ryan Publishing, 1990)

Philip, Neil: *The Penguin Book of Scottish Folktales* (London: Penguin Books, 1995)

Rhys, John: *Celtic Folklore, Welsh and Manx* (Oxford: The Clarendon Press, 1901)

Robertson, R. Macdonald: *Selected Highland Folktales, gathered orally* (Newton Abbot: David & Charles, 1977)

Stewart, William G.: *The popular superstitions and festive amusements of the Highlanders of Scotland* (Edinburgh: printed for Archibald Constable and Company, and Hurst, Robinson and Co. London, 1823)

Stokes, Whitley (translator): 'The Irish Ordeals, Cormac's Adventure in the Land of Promise, and the Decision as to Cormac's Sword', in *Irische Texte, Ser. III.1*, (Leipzig: Hirzel, 1891)

Thomas, W. Jenkyn: *The Welsh Fairy Book* (New York: F.A. Stokes, 1908)

Yeats, W.B. (editor): *The Book of Fairy and Folk Tales of Ireland* (Originally published in two volumes: 'Fairy and Folk Tales of the Irish Peasantry',1888; and 'Irish Fairy Tales', 1892 (London: The Slaney Press, 1994)

Picture Credits

p.2 © British Library Board. All Rights Reserved / Bridgeman Images. Illustrated by Warwick Goble; p.9 ©Chronicle / Alamy Stock Photo. Illustrated by J. R. Skelton; p.10 ©Bridgeman Images. Illustrated by Harry George Theaker; p.13 ©Bridgeman Images. Illustrated by Eric Ennion; p.18 © Historic Illustrations / Alamy Stock Photo. Illustrated by Arthur Rackham; p.21 © Album / Alamy Stock Photo. Illustrated by E. Wallcousins; p.25 © Mouseion Archives / Alamy Stock Photo. Illustrated by Walter Crane; p.27 Public domain. Illustrated by Walter Crane; p.29. © Timewatch Images / Alamy Stock Photo. Illustrated by Hugh Thomsom; p.32. © Look and Learn / Bridgeman Images. Illustrated by Richard Doyle; p.39. Public domain. Illustrated by Alice B Woodward; p.40. Public domain. Illustrator unknown; p.46 © AF Fotografie / Alamy Stock Photo. Illustrated by Arthur Rackham; p.49. Public domain. Illustrated by Stephen Reid; p.52. © Painters / Alamy Stock Photo. Illustrated by Arthur Rackham; p.58. © Heritage Image Partnership Ltd. / Alamy Stock Photo. Illustrated by Stephen Reid, p.61 © ClassicStock / Alamy Stock Photo. Illustrated by Monro S. Orr; p.62 © past art / Alamy Stock Photo. Illustrated by Marjory P Rhodes; p.64 Public domain. Illustrated by Morris Meredith Williams; p.67 Public domain. Illustrated by Claude Arthur Shepperson; p.70 Public domain/Alamy Stock Photo. Illustrated by Maurice Lalau; p.73 © Lebrecht Authors / Bridgeman Images. Illustrated by Harry George Theaker; p.78 © Look and Learn / Bridgeman Images. Illustrated by Harry George Theaker; p.81 © Lebrecht Authors / Bridgeman Images. Illustrated by Harry George Theaker; p.83 © Mary Evans Picture Library. Illustrated by an unnamed artist (signed 'H.D.'); p.89 © Hilary Morgan / Alamy Stock Photo. Illustrated by Arthur Rackham; p.90 © Archives Charmet / Bridgeman Images. Illustrated by Ivan Bilibin; p.95 © Mary Evans Picture Library. Illustrated by P Lackerbauer; p.96 © sharpner / Alamy Stock Photo; p.102 © hilwissedition Ltd. && Co. KG / Alamy Stock Photo. Illustrated by Gustave Dore; p.105 © markku murto/art / Alamy Stock Photo. Illustrated by Wilhelm Kuhnert; p.108 © GraphicaArtis / Bridgeman Images. Illustrated by Pierre Jacques Smit; p.110 © iStockPhoto. Illustrated by R. Bowlder Sharp; p.113 © Look and Learn / Elgar Collection / Bridgeman Images. Illustrator unknown, p.114 © Egle Lipeikaite / Alamy Stock Photo. Illustrator unknown; p.117 © iStockPhoto. Illustrated by Gustave Dore; p.122 © Vera Petruk / Alamy Stock Vector; p.124 © Heritage Image Partnership Ltd / Alamy Stock Photo. Illustrated by Stephen Reid; p.127 © Giancarlo Costa / Bridgeman Images. Illustrated by Arthur Rackham; p.130 © Hristo Chernev / Alamy Stock Photo; p.133 Public domain. Illustrated by Warner Mole; p.136 © Susan Isakson / Alamy Stock Photo. Illustrated by Warwick Goble; p.139 © Lanmas / Alamy Stock Photo. Illustrated by Juan Scherr; p.144 Public domain. Illustrated by Morris Meredith Williams; p.147 KG / Alamy Stock Photo. Illustrator unknown; p.149 © Christie's Images / Bridgeman Images. Illustrated by William Holbrook Beard; p.150 © Patrick Guenette / Alamy Stock Photo. Illustrator unknown; p.153 © Bridgeman Images. Illustrated by Arthur C. Michael; p.158 Public domain / Alamy Stock Photo. Illustrated by A. Birrel and J. W. Upham; p.161 Public domain. Illustrated by Morris Meredith Williams; p.166 Public domain. Illustrated by John D. Batten; p.170 Public domain. Illustrated by John D. Batten; p.173 Public domain. Illustrated by John Duncan; p.147 p.180 Public domain. Illustrated by Beatrice Elvery; p.183 Public domain / Alamy Stock Photo. Illustrator unknown; p.208 Heritage Image Partnership Ltd / Alamy Stock Photo. Illustrated by Arthur Joseph Gaskin.

Other Books by
Rosalind Kerven

Dark Fairy Tales of Fearless Women
Medieval Legends of Love & Lust
Native American Myths
Viking Myths & Sagas
Faeries, Elves & Goblins: The Old Stories
Arthurian Legends
English Fairy Tales and Legends